She caressed him all over with her hands...

Taking in the smooth feel of Clint's skin, Margot wanted to touch and taste and lick and suck every sweet morsel. The simple touch wasn't enough. Nothing seemed like enough as she tried to absorb every sensation she could.

His fingers came around the left strap of her thong and in one quick yank he snapped it off as though it were nothing. He tossed it over his shoulder and worked his way down.

"You drive me wild," he ~~~~~~~~~ digging his teeth into the sensiti~~~~~~~~~ thigh. Then his tongue d~~~~~~~~~ his lips and...

Blaze

Dear Reader,

After writing several books featuring deliciously dark and wounded heroes, I was aching to write a romance involving a fun and flirty playboy. Thus Clint Hilton was born. He's rich. He's funny. He's gorgeous, and he's got the world at his fingertips. Now all he needs is a nice, sensible woman to round out his good fortune. And when he hires matchmaker Margot Roth to find a date for his mother, that's exactly what he gets.

While I enjoyed writing this fun and flirty couple, one of my favorite aspects of this book was the many secondary characters I was able to include. I have the overbearing mother, a young and irresponsible college frat boy and the lively best friend, who brings with her a culture of warm family and big hearts. Throw in a few lovelorn clients who have romance troubles of their own and you've got a group of people who unwittingly conspire to bring this couple together.

I hope you enjoy the book as much as I enjoyed writing it. Please drop me a note at www.LoriBorrill.com and tell me what you think of it.

Happy reading!

Lori Borrill

The Personal Touch

LORI BORRILL

TORONTO • NEW YORK • LONDON
AMSTERDAM • PARIS • SYDNEY • HAMBURG
STOCKHOLM • ATHENS • TOKYO • MILAN • MADRID
PRAGUE • WARSAW • BUDAPEST • AUCKLAND

Recycling programs
for this product may
not exist in your area.

ISBN-13: 978-0-373-79488-1

THE PERSONAL TOUCH

www.eHarlequin.com

Printed in U.S.A.

ABOUT THE AUTHOR

An Oregon native, Lori Borrill moved to the Bay Area just out of high school and has been a transplanted Californian ever since. Her weekdays are spent at the insurance company where she's been employed for more than twenty years, and she credits her writing career to the unending help and support she receives from her husband and real-life hero. When not sitting in front of a computer, she can usually be found at the Little League fields playing proud parent to their son. She'd love to hear from readers, and can be reached through her Web site at www.LoriBorrill.com.

Books by Lori Borrill

HARLEQUIN BLAZE
308—PRIVATE CONFESSIONS
344—UNDERNEATH IT ALL*
392—PUTTING IT TO THE TEST
430—UNLEASHED

*Million Dollar Secrets

To Elle Kennedy and Tracy Wolff.
Writers need friends, and you two are the best.

To Wanda, the sweetest one
in our crazy bunch.

For Al and Tommy

1

WHEN THE FASHION industry's hottest cover model flashed her signature *do-me* smile and stepped out of her black silk dress, Clint Hilton decided this was one sultry beauty that had definitely been worth waiting for.

If you could call three weeks a wait.

In Clint's book of sexual conquests, it was a millennium. A week more than he'd waited for any other woman and as long as he'd gone without sex in recent memory. But ever since the two had met in Vegas last month, he'd wanted a taste of this dish. And when she'd said she was leaving for Milan that night, she'd asked him for the one thing that trumped his need for fast and frequent flings.

She'd asked him to make a promise. Wait for her to get back from her trip.

Only three tiny little weeks. Her in Italy shooting perfume ads and him in Los Angeles, cooling his cock in the Pacific Ocean while he tried to remember how he let a woman put his sex life on hold.

He couldn't recall what had made him agree. Maybe it was the barely-there dress she'd worn that night. More likely the look in her eye that said she was worth it. But nonetheless, he'd honored his word. He had to. It was one of the few things he cherished more than having a good time.

She stepped to the edge of the pool, nothing covering that

caramel skin except for the lacy red thong that topped her long, slender legs. Behind her, the view over West Hollywood nearly stretched to the ocean on this exceptionally clear night. But though he loved to relax on his terrace, tonight wouldn't be spent gazing at the city below. Tonight was payback time. Three long weeks of celibacy ending by the graces of one tall, stunning cover model named Rachelle.

No last name. "Just Rachelle," she'd said.

Damn, if that wasn't sexy.

With that smoky look holding promise in her eyes, she tossed the last of her clothes, flung her hands over her head and dove into the pool. Her slender form moved fluidly through the water, inching toward him like a shark coming in for the kill. And as she neared, she stroked her hands up his legs and trailed her tongue along his shaft, breaking through the surface in a series of slippery kisses that hardened his cock and weakened his knees.

Their mouths met hot and deep, like they had back in Vegas, and he sucked in the scent of chlorine and expensive perfume. Her lips still held the essence of the Cosmopolitan she'd left on the terrace, and while her tongue did a number on his senses, she coiled her legs around his thighs and began to grind against his erection. It nearly broke him in half. He was too ready for this night. And as if to torture him more, she broke the kiss to whisper all the things she planned to do with him.

Sexy things. Naughty things. Things most women didn't care for and a gentleman never requested. But Rachelle wasn't looking for a gentleman tonight. She was here to prove that when it came to judging people, Clint Hilton was head of the class.

It was one of the skills he'd inherited from his father, what put him on top in his game and what had him darting through a casino full of beautiful women to that one special blonde by the bar. The one with the eyes of steam.

Clint could always spot the difference between real bedroom eyes and ones only learned for the camera. And Rachelle was the genuine article. She was the stuff wet dreams were made of, the kind of sex kitten that made suave men babble and bungling boys faint.

And tonight she was all his.

She glanced over his shoulder and smiled. "I see you've lit the fireplace in your bedroom. It looks cozy."

He had. Not that April in Los Angeles was especially chilly. He'd simply gone to painstaking efforts to make sure everything was perfect tonight, starting with dinner on the beach and ending with cocktails by the pool. The lighting was timed to take over when the sun finally set. Low jazz hummed throughout the house. The tables were set with flowers and fresh citrus and the bars had been fully restocked.

And, of course, he had condoms tucked around every corner, in arm's reach of any room, bed and surface that might spark Rachelle's fancy. Given some of the plans she just shared, Clint suspected that endeavor hadn't been in vain.

He lifted her high around his waist and began suckling her breast. "Would you like to move inside?"

Her quiet laugh held pure sin. "It might be safer. I'd hate to see you drown before I get my fill."

He moved his lips to the other breast. "I'm a very good swimmer."

Droplets of water slid from her hair and trickled down her chest, and he started a game of catching them with his tongue before they hit the water's edge.

"You know," she said, her breath getting heavy as he lifted her higher and moved his mouth down her waist, "you could probably get me started right here." Then with the swiftness of a cat, she pushed from his arms, lifted herself to the side of the pool and spread her thighs wide with invitation.

His heart thumped and his erection hardened. He cupped his hands around the pool's edge and moved between her legs. Through the chlorine and the sweet scent of star jasmine, the smell of sex filled his nostrils, putting an ache in his crotch as he began kissing her tender folds. She inched closer and spread wider, tossing her wet blond hair over her shoulder to stop the pat-pat-pat of droplets on her thighs. Then as he slowly circled her clit, she threw her head back and moaned.

"That's it, stud. Show me what you've got."

He blew hot breath on her nub and began the feast, licking her sensitive spots and then slipping his tongue into her core. Her muscles clenched and his cock twitched, the idea of getting inside that tight space nearly taking him to the edge. But it was far from time. She had too many plans—plans he really, really liked. So he worked hard to focus on her pleasure and keep his own in check.

Faster, he stroked. Her toes tapped against the water as her sex slickened and swelled. And with a low cry that started deep in her chest and echoed down the canyon, she came apart.

Her climax pushed his need to the point of pain. Even the cool water of the pool did nothing to temper the throb. And when she rose to her feet and told him to come inside, he nearly stumbled over himself as he pushed out of the pool and followed.

"I need your cock now," she casually remarked.

"At your service."

He grabbed her hand and pulled her into a long, greedy kiss, forcing himself to take his time and savor every moment. But just as he was about to break the kiss and lead her to his bedroom, the click of the gate and a sharp yelp from the side of the house startled them both to attention.

"Oh! I…"

Clint looked up. "Mom!"

Rachelle darted for a towel.

At the gate to the side yard, his mother stood agape dressed in tidy khaki chinos, a pale blue cardigan and pearl stud earrings. Brown leather sandals matched her purse, and she stood on the grass, her mouth silently bobbing, pointing a finger toward a hydrangea bush.

"Pom Pom," she finally uttered, referring to the dog he'd given her for Christmas.

Clint grabbed a towel of his own and stood next to Rachelle, whose flushed cheeks had morphed from arousal to embarrassment.

"What the hell are you doing home?" he asked. "You're supposed to be in Palm Springs."

"I—" his mother started, but before she could finish, he heard the flattened tone of his date.

"You live with your *mother?*"

"Huh?" He turned and looked at Rachelle. Her embarrassment was gone. So was that smoky bedroom look in her eyes, replaced by the bland and somewhat disbelieving look of a woman unimpressed.

"No, my mother lives with *me.*"

She responded with an expression he didn't like.

"It's entirely different," he affirmed.

"If you say so." She headed toward her clothes.

"I'm serious. This is *my* house."

"And you share it with your mother."

"What's wrong with that?" he asked. But he already knew what was wrong with that. He'd been trying to get Jillian Hilton to move out pretty much ever since he'd offered to let her stay with him after his father died. The situation was supposed to be temporary, a month or two while she got over her grief and learned to live on her own. And yes, more than a year later she was still here. And yes, she was driving him nuts. But she was his mother. With his only brother being a news correspondent traveling through the Middle East, what was he supposed to do?

"Nothing's wrong with that," Rachelle said in a tone that said otherwise.

"Now, wait a minute. My mother's leaving." He turned a stern eye to Jillian to express that was an order, not a suggestion. She'd had plans. They'd arranged this. She was off for the weekend with her best friend, Marge, leaving him here—*alone*—for a night filled with lots of overdue sex.

But Rachelle simply kept walking, shaking her head as she gathered her purse and clothes.

"Yes," his mother said. "I am leaving. I just—Pom Pom, no!" She rushed to the side of the hill but it was too late. Pom Pom, his mother's precious Pomeranian and Clint's royal pain in the ass, had darted down the hill. And being that the dog had a mind of its own, Clint knew it wasn't coming back any time soon.

Tying his towel tightly around his waist, he stepped toward the edge of the hill, hoping the dog might be within reach, but the puffed-up furball had crept under a bush. "Great." He turned back to his mother. "You still haven't answered my question."

"I *am* leaving," his mother tried, but Rachelle had already pulled out her phone and was calling a cab.

He stepped back to his date. "What are you doing?"

"I'm sorry. This isn't going to work at all."

His mother attempted to call her dog.

"What isn't going to work?" he asked, becoming slightly annoyed by the impatient look on her face. "I told you, my mother is leaving."

Rachelle snorted, snapped her phone closed and tucked it in her purse. "I thought you were a little more...*indepen-*

dent?" Then she began walking toward the house, holding her clothes in her hand and the towel around her chest. "Really, Clint. If I'd known you were still tied to the apron strings, I wouldn't have wasted my time."

Okay, now he was pissed.

"Apron strings?"

His mother gasped. "My son is no such thing!"

Nice gesture, but his mom defending him right now was definitely bad timing.

"Thanks for dinner. I'll have a car send your towel back later," Rachelle said.

"Really, I'm sorry," his mother tried, but Clint was one step past apologies.

Crossing his arms over his chest, he watched with amazement as Rachelle hurried to the door. "You've got to be kidding."

Rachelle simply looked at Jillian, then back at him. "You two enjoy your evening."

"Wait—" Jillian attempted, but Clint shot up a hand. He wasn't sure who he was angrier with, his mom for coming home when she knew he had a date, or Rachelle for being so quick to dash off—after he'd waited *three weeks* for her.

Right now it was a toss-up, though Mom would surely win the bonus round if he had to go traipsing through scrub brush chasing after the damn dog.

Jillian stood with her mouth open, watching Rachelle disappear into the house on her way to the front door.

"Well, now that you've ruined my evening, would you finally answer my question?" he growled. "You were supposed to have left with Marge hours ago."

When they heard the distant slam of the front door, she snapped her mouth shut and turned her eyes to him. All signs of remorse were gone; instead, his mother looked aghast.

"Well," she huffed. "If that's all it takes to ruin an evening, what does she do on a *bad* date? Pull out an Uzi and start firing?"

"Why are you here?"

She clamped her hands to her hips. "Honestly, Clint, I don't know where you find these women. Do you actually think you can have a relationship with someone like that?"

He hadn't been looking for a relationship. He just wanted some really hot sex. But instead of pointing that out, he opted to skip to the obvious.

"You embarrassed the hell out of her—out of *us*. Do you have any idea what you walked in on?"

"The same thing that goes on here every time I leave for the weekend. And they're all the same, shallow and self-centered. Did your father and I set such a horrible example that you can't even consider dating a woman who might actually make a good wife?"

"You and Dad were great." And it was true. His parents had a wonderful marriage. Which was what had devastated his mother so when his father died. They'd been perfect for each other. Like peas and carrots. And someday, Clint would love to have what they had. He just wasn't in a hurry.

"Then why can't you bring home someone kind and intelligent for a change?"

His eyes narrowed. "You keep avoiding my question. What happened to your weekend in Palm Springs?"

His mother let out a breath and plopped down in one of the stuffed chairs at the covered end of the terrace. "Marge and I had a difference of opinion."

"You got in a fight." What a shock. It had been happening since the two women had met back in grade school.

He should have known.

"She wanted to bring a date! It was supposed to be the two

of us, and at the last minute, she announced she was bringing some guy named Arnie along."

Clint stepped to the bar he kept stocked in the outdoor kitchen and poured himself two fingers of scotch. It was looking as though his entire weekend was about to be shot.

"And the worst of it all," his mother went on. "Do you know where she found this man?"

Knowing Marge, it could have been anywhere. The woman was on her fourth divorce. Or was it five?

He shrugged.

"A dating service!"

"What's wrong with a dating service?"

That blanched look returned to her face. "It's the final stage of desperation, that's what. You know those places are only for social misfits."

"Mom, I hardly think that's fair. Lots of people use dating services these days—" He stopped and stared. "Wait a minute. Did you *tell* her that?"

"Of course. She's my friend. If I don't look out for her, who will? She should appreciate my candor instead of swearing me out of her life."

Oh, beautiful. Another Hilton-Dawson feud. The last one had lasted four months and that was over a sweater from Nordstrom's. If she and Marge were headed for another big one, that meant his mother would be hanging around bored again. And if there was one thing worse than living with his mother, it was living with his bored mother.

He slugged back his drink. "No. Oh, no. You call up Marge and apologize."

"Over my dead body."

It just might come to that. Seriously. He hadn't known how a five-thousand-square-foot home could end up too small for two people, but it was. It had been barely tolerable having to schedule his social life around the comings and goings of his mom. It would be worse if she stopped going entirely. After all, it wasn't as though he could just leave her here and not come home. When she got lonely, she got depressed. When she got depressed, she started looking for things to bother herself about. And when she started looking, his life became a living hell no matter where he was.

No, he'd learned all that the hard way. The best thing for his mom had been Marge, and if she was out of the picture indefinitely, he'd need to find someone besides himself to fill the gap.

His mother rose and poured herself a glass of wine. "No. Marge is making a big mistake with this man, and when she finds that out, she'll be the one apologizing to me."

Clint snorted. Marge was the only woman more stubborn than his mom. He doubted she'd ever apologized for anything.

"In the meantime, my Palm Springs weekend is off." Then she finally showed a sign of apology. "I'm sorry about your date. I had really been trying to sneak up to my room unnoticed. But you left the side gate open and Pom Pom flew through before I could catch her."

The gentleman in him pressed him to say it was all right, but the sex-deprived bachelor wouldn't let him. Right now, he was supposed to be working on his second orgasm, just the thought of which had him grinding his teeth so hard he nearly split a filling. He didn't need apologies. He needed a good hard screaming climax with a beautiful blond bombshell to wipe away three weeks of anticipation and pent-up steam.

Instead, he had an irked and lonely mother and her puffed-up, oversized rat.

Hardly the life of a swinging single bachelor.

Setting his empty glass on the granite counter, he moved

toward his bedroom to symbolically shut off the fire. "I'm going to drive down to the coast for a swim."

"In the ocean? I don't understand why you go all the way down there when you've got a perfectly good swimming pool right in your backyard."

He slid open the glass door, flattened his lips and grumbled, "Water's colder."

2

"SHE'S DRIVING ME crazy."

Clint was stretched out on the couch in the reception area of his Wilshire Boulevard office. For the last twenty minutes, he'd been spilling his problems to his office manager, Carmen Padilla, as though she were his personal shrink. After four years with his firm, it had become one of her unofficial job titles.

"Your mother's not that bad," she attempted.

She sat behind her large reception desk, the Bluetooth receiver a permanent fixture to her ear, while she listened to Clint's woes.

"Do you know how I spent my weekend?"

"From what you've told me so far, I'm almost afraid to ask."

"My mother and I toured health clubs for two days."

"I thought she just joined one."

"She did. With her ex-friend Marge. Now she insists on finding a new club so they don't accidentally run into each other." He pushed up from the couch and began circling the marble tiled floor. "Forget the fact that I've got a gym right in my own house. And the fact that she just paid a year's membership at Rolling Hills. *And* the fact that in the end, she'll go for two weeks, then find some reason to never go back again. I still spent my weekend touring every health club in Hollywood."

He stopped and looked at Carmen. "Do you know how many health clubs there are around here?"

She shrugged and blinked her eyes innocently, though her smirk admitted evil pleasure in this. Having a large and close family, Carmen held little sympathy for Clint's situation. "More than three?"

"You don't care at all, do you?"

"Of course I do," she insisted, but the grin said she was lying. Carmen's family was tight-knit. The children stayed close to the nest and relatives were as much friends as family. And to Clint's credit, he'd had the same relationship with his own family back when his father was his business partner and his brother wrote local stories for the *L.A. Times*.

But when his dad died suddenly of a heart attack, all that changed. For a while, his brother, Nate, had stayed with their mother, helping her through her grief while Clint dealt with the family's contracting business. The arrangement got them all through the shock of their father's death until Nate got the opportunity of a lifetime with an assignment that took him to Afghanistan. It was thrilling for Nate, but terrifying for their mother, who feared losing a son after her husband. And in the end, Clint was left holding all the bags. It was often that Clint thought of the other men in his family as if they'd abandoned him. And days like this, the taste was especially bitter.

Carmen must have seen the look on his face because her playful edge sobered.

"Okay, let's tackle this like any other business matter," she said. "Your mother's bored and you're all she's got." She tapped her pen on the dark cherrywood desk and thought for a while. "You need to find her someone else to play with."

"I already bought her a dog."

"I was thinking more along the lines of a new man."

He turned the idea over in his mind. "I'm listening."

"Trust me. I know women. If your mom had a lover, *she'd* be the one complaining that you're hanging around too much."

He wondered if his mother was ready for it. It had been almost two years since his father died. She was past her stage of mourning. Had even mentioned on one or two occasions the thought of entering the dating world again—in a fearful kind of way, but Clint knew that meant she'd been thinking about it.

"How about your uncle, Gabe?" he asked.

Carmen frowned. "Gabe doesn't speak English."

"I'm not picky."

"You need to be. The wrong man could make everything worse."

"I don't need worse," he agreed.

"You need Margot." She jotted a note on a pad and handed it to him.

"Who's Margot?"

"My friend and only the best dating counselor in West L.A."

"Oh, no. My mother will never agree to a dating service." He shook his head with conviction. "Even if I could brighten her opinion of matchmakers, she wouldn't see one now after the fight she had with Marge. It would be like admitting Marge was right, and Mom's way too stubborn for that." He crumpled the paper in his hand and tossed it back to Carmen. "Sorry. I need a Plan B."

She took the note and smoothed it back out. "Talk to her anyway. I'm serious. She's the one who got Nico and me together without even trying, and she's got plenty of clients your mother's age. If you talk to her, I'm sure the two of you will figure something out."

He scoffed. "My weekend was destroyed thanks to my mother and her opinions about matchmakers."

"Margot's not just a matchmaker. She's a counselor for singles. Your mom doesn't even need to know you've spoken with her. Just seek her out for the advice." She handed the note back to Clint. "Aren't you the one who always said if you want a job done right, hire a professional?"

"I was referring to construction."

"It's true for everything. Your mom needs a new man in her life. Margot can tell you how to make that happen."

Clint stared at the wrinkled page. Though a year ago he would have felt otherwise, the thought of his mother remarried to a nice guy now seemed like a dream come true. He'd love to have things back the way they used to be, her busy with her own life and him enjoying his. But Carmen was right. His mother had already been through enough. He didn't want to see her hurt all over again by a dating game that could often be cruel and dangerous. Heck, the last time the woman was single, Jimmy Carter was president. Things had changed.

"Trust me," Carmen said. "You won't be sorry."

"Famous last words." But he tucked the note in his pocket anyway. He had to do something to fix this situation before his relationship with his mother was ruined forever. And the way things were going, that's exactly where this would end.

"SHE MADE this funny noise when we had sex."

Margot Roth stared at her client, not sure she wanted him to elaborate on that comment. The woman he was talking about had been Margot's hairstylist for years and this conversation bordered on TMI—*too much information*. Not that Margot hadn't had discussions like this before. To be successful as a dating counselor, she'd often had to peel back the layers of a client's most intimate issues. She only wondered if she could sit for two hours every eight weeks having her highlights retouched knowing these kinds of details about her stylist, Gail.

Curiosity got the best of her.

"What kind of funny noise?"

He wrinkled his nose. "Sort of a…whistle in her nose… kind of a growling thing…" He checked his perfectly manicured fingernails. "Maybe a clicking kind of thing."

She stared at him blankly. "Well, what is it, David? A whistle, growl or a click?"

He sucked in a big breath and let it out. "Maybe all three, maybe none. I don't know." He tossed his head to the side to whip the dark bangs from his eyes, and when Margot fell silent and waited for a more solid answer, he rose to his feet and began pacing.

David was clearly anxious and frustrated. This was the third woman Margot had paired him with, each one more perfect for him than the last, yet something kept holding him back. And after six weeks of getting to know him, digging deeper and deeper into his psyche, Margot was almost certain she knew what it was. She just didn't know if he was ready to hear it.

"David," she said. "How do you feel about Gail on a personal level?"

He stopped his pacing and smiled brightly. "Oh, she's great. Every time we're together we talk all night. You're totally right about her. In fact, I scored some tickets to the Indie Film Festival next month and I've asked her to go with me. We'll have a blast."

"It's only on an intimate level that you aren't quite connecting."

He seemed relieved that she understood. "Exactly. I just don't feel *that way* about her, and I don't know how to tell her."

"You have to be honest with her. And don't waste time doing it. If you truly value her friendship and want it to continue, you've got to be kind but frank about this. Leading her on will only make things worse when the truth does come out."

It was advice Margot often doled out. She was a stickler about open communication when it came to relationships, and she wasn't above canceling a contract with a client who couldn't be honest with his or her partner.

"I don't want to lead her on. But I was kind of hoping maybe you could talk to—"

Margot shook her head before he could finish the sentence. "She needs to hear it from you." Then she gave him a reassuring smile. "Besides, I know you can do it. You're a kind, gentle man, David. You'll find the right way to talk to her about this and everything will be fine."

That is, everything will be fine between David and Gail. Getting to the bottom of David's intimacy issues in general would be a little touchier.

Though Margot had a bachelor's degree in counseling and psychology, she wasn't trained to handle the deeper emotional issues she sometimes ran into in her line of work. Usually, once she suspected there was more going on with a client than the need to learn some social skills or find the right companion, she referred them to one of the many trained professionals she had on file.

And after this date with Gale, Margot debated whether David was one of those candidates.

"You're right," he said. "I can talk to her. And I will. But…" he bit his lip. "Where does that leave us? I mean, I'm really looking for a soul mate, and Gail isn't it."

Nor was any other woman, if Margot's suspicions were correct. And they usually were. With David, it had taken her a couple dates to figure out that he might be struggling with his sexuality. And now, after his date with Gail, she was sure of it. She only hesitated wondering whether or not he was ready to face the truth.

She pursed her lips and studied him, looking for some kind of sign that might tell her how he'd react to the suggestion he might be gay. There was such an innocence about him, an almost boyish sweetness that had her caring more for his feelings than for their business relationship. She didn't want to throw reality in his face if he wasn't prepared to consider it.

"You know, actually," he finally said, "some guys I know are going down to Cabo for a long weekend. They've asked me to go along."

"What kind of guys?" The question slipped from her lips before she could consider the insinuation in it.

"A guy I know from work and a few of his friends."

She waited for him to elaborate, and when he didn't, she simply said, "Sounds like fun."

He nodded. "Yeah. Yeah, it will be. And I was thinking maybe we'd put off any more dates until after I get back from this trip."

A sense of relief eased the tension in Margot's shoulders. Maybe David *was* ready to explore the truth.

"I think that's a great idea."

He looked as though he was about to say something else, but then he rose to his feet instead. "I'll call Gail tonight."

Margot stood with him. "I know you two will be fine," she assured him. In truth, she'd already spoken with Gail and the two women had come to the same conclusion. He'd make a great friend, but when it came to life partners, he was probably drafting from the wrong team.

She followed him out to the reception area of the office she shared with her partner, Alan Immendorf. She and Alan together owned Intimates, a full-service relationship counseling center for men and women who've had trouble finding that special person. Most of the time, their clients were people who, because of their careers or other obligations, didn't have the time to go searching the usual places for a date. Many didn't know where to go or how to approach the opposite sex. And then others needed deeper help in understanding themselves and getting real about the type of person they were looking for—David being an extreme example.

And though it was the latter group she usually had the most trouble with, they could also be the most rewarding. The ones she truly felt would have spent the bulk of their lives frustrated and confused if it weren't for the help she provided.

Margot had been a romantic her whole life. Couple that with a keen instinct when it came to people and she'd found quick success in her choice of profession. And when she paired up with Alan, her gay business partner who handled many of their clients with alternative lifestyles, the two had come together to create what was becoming one of the more notable firms in their field.

"So you'll call me when you get back from Cabo," she said as she led David through the reception area toward the front door. "I think the trip will be good for you. I'm looking forward to hearing how it went."

He smiled. "I will." And when he walked out onto the street, she knew for certain the man who came back would be changed.

"When are you going to hand him over?"

She jumped at Alan's voice behind her. "What were you doing, lurking behind the palms? You scared the daylights out of me."

"I heard your voices and came to see how it went. Were you and Gail right?"

"I'm guessing if he returns as a client, it will be as one of yours instead of mine."

She told Alan about her meeting with David and his upcoming trip to Cabo San Lucas, and when she was done, Alan regarded her with a cocky grin. "I told you he wasn't just metrosexual."

"Oh, stop acting like you've got a sixth sense. Your gaydar didn't go off any sooner than mine did."

"No, but I'll be happy to steal your client if he still needs our services."

"I'm thinking he won't, but if I'm wrong, he's all yours."

Alan laughed and handed her a note. "This call came into the main line during your appointment. Some guy named Clint Hilton. Carmen referred him to you."

"That's her boss. Did he say what he wanted?"

"Your services, apparently."

Margot stared at the paper in her hand. Though she'd never met Carmen's boss, she'd heard plenty about him and found it highly implausible he'd need a dating counselor. From what she understood, the man had no problem finding women.

"I can't see why. He doesn't fit the profile."

"Well, you're about to find out. He'll be here any minute."

"What?"

"He had another appointment in the neighborhood and wanted to drop by afterward. I told him you were in but I couldn't guarantee you'd be available." When Alan noted the quizzical look in her eye, he added, "You can hide out in your office if you want me to get rid of him."

"No, I don't mind talking with him. I'm just caught a little off guard, is all. I would have liked to have talked with Carmen first to see what this is about."

"So go call her. If he shows up, I'll have him wait. My next appointment isn't for a while."

"Maybe I will."

But before she could duck into her office, she heard the front door open.

Margot had never seen Clint Hilton before, but based on the stories she'd heard from Carmen, she knew with all certainty the tall, drop-dead sexy man approaching them was him.

He strolled in with the casual ease of a man accustomed to dominating the space around him. Relaxed and calm, as though he could find common ground with a mechanic or a millionaire banker alike. His shoulders were broad and his hands worn. He wasn't simply the paper-pushing end of the contracting business he owned, and the sun-kissed highlights in his dirty blond hair didn't come from a bottle.

He was the genuine article. A West L.A. version of the Marlboro Man, if such a thing existed.

A dark pair of Armanis covered his eyes and his brown leather Oxfords were unmistakably Santoni. Along with the stainless steel Rolex, business-casual slacks and tailored dress shirt, she guessed he was wearing a fortune worth more than her car. Yet there was nothing stuffy or presumptuous about his appearance. He wore the ensemble as though he'd thrown it on the same way the rest of the world slipped into a pair of sweats and sneakers.

As the door closed behind him he smiled, revealing a set of perfectly white teeth. His grin pressed dimples into the strong hollows of his cheeks and set off a chain reaction she felt straight to her toes. And when he pulled off his shades, the gaze from his deep blue eyes seemed to slip straight under her skin, sending a shiver through her veins that stole her speech and garbled her thoughts.

She stood there gaping while Alan held out a hand in her rescue. "You must be Clint Hilton. We spoke on the phone."

Clint turned the lethal smile away, allowing her to momentarily catch her breath and recollect some basic facts—like her name.

What was wrong with her? Rich and handsome men walked into their offices all the time, yet today she stood there like an awed, giddy groupie. She lied and told herself it was resonant fluster from her meeting with David. Or maybe her blood sugar was low, the blueberry muffin she'd had for breakfast coming back to haunt her.

That had to explain the light-headed dizziness that had just come over her because either of those things was better than admitting an instant crush on her best friend's boss.

"Yes, I'm Clint." He shook Alan's hand with vigor. "Alan, good to meet you."

Tucking his sunglasses into his shirt pocket, he turned the hand to Margot. "Margot Roth?" When she nodded, he added, "Carmen regards you very highly."

She accepted the handshake while mentally pulling herself together. If Clint had come seeking her professional services, now wasn't the time to act like a babbling idiot.

"If this is a bad time, I can make an appointment," he offered. "I'm renovating a building over on 6th and happened to be in the area."

"The old Fuller building. I'm familiar with it," she managed to utter.

He quirked a smile that said he was impressed and she marveled over why that excited her so.

He's just a man. An incredibly sexy man. And in case you've forgotten, you've already found Mr. Wonderful.

The memory of Rob, the man she'd started dating a month ago, brought her feet back down to earth. Now, Rob was the man she should be getting silly over. Perfect for her in every way.

And as a woman in the business of forming lasting relationships, she should know.

So she did her best to set her lust aside and get to work. "I've got time. If you'd like, we could meet now."

He slapped his big hands together. "Great. I'm anxious to see what you can do for me."

His choice of words sparked a number of inappropriate responses, but she held them all in check, insistent on shaking off this strange reaction of hers.

Rob, think of Rob, she thought. And money. Lots of money. A new client always made for a good day, and with a heavy mortgage on a brand-new condo, she could use all the business she could get.

So with those thoughts firmly fixed in her mind, she set off down the hall to find out exactly what she could do for the sexy Clint Hilton.

3

MARGOT ROTH was cute. That was the impression that lingered in Clint's mind as he stood in her downtown office with her and her partner, Alan. Her round face complemented a wide mouth and big brown eyes. She was shorter than average, Clint doubted she'd hit five-five in three-inch heels, and her figure was curved and fleshy. Definitely girl-next-door with her shoulder-length brown hair and bright, unassuming smile. Nothing like the tall, chiseled beauties he typically gravitated to.

Which was why it puzzled him that he couldn't seem to keep his eyes off her.

He followed as she moved toward a short corridor and down the hall, his gaze continually dipping to the bottom half of her hourglass figure. He liked the way it looked wrapped up in those coffee-brown slacks—shapely and touchable, firm but entirely feminine. Her legs were lengthened by high-heeled sandals that had something sparkly on them, like rhinestones or glitter, and her white ruffled blouse topped her off like whipped cream on a hot fudge sundae.

"Have a seat," he heard her say, and it was only then he realized they'd actually entered her office. He quickly darted his eyes somewhere respectable before she caught him gawking and labeled him a perv. He didn't typically give every woman the full Hilton once-over, but then again, it wasn't every woman who flew into his radar like Margot Roth had.

Taking in his surroundings, he was surprised by the antique furniture in her office. The reception area had been ultra contemporary with bright-colored sofas, tall, sleek palms and bold canvas artwork. This room was like stepping into another world. A large mahogany table took the place of her desk. Queen Anne, if he knew his furniture. And she'd played the rest of the room off it with an antique sideboard subbing for a credenza, large, chunky bookcases framing the back wall and a deep burgundy Persian rug defining the space.

It occurred to him that it fit her, rich and textured, comfortable and calm, and the more he saw of Ms. Roth, the more she intrigued him.

She gestured to one of the two cushioned chairs facing her, and he took the one closest, edging it away from the table to give room for his long frame. After she'd gathered a pad and pen, she smiled and asked, "So how can I help you, Mr. Hilton?"

He cleared his throat and tried to recall why he was there— a minute detail that seemed to have slipped his mind in the short moments between his car and her office.

"My mother," he said. "She's in need of a companion." Then he added abruptly, "A *male* companion."

She winked. "I'd assumed as much since we don't breed dogs here."

His laugh was heartier than it should have been. "I tried that one already. Now I've got a bored mother *and* a dog."

"So she's looking for a gentleman now."

"Well, she's not exactly looking. I am. I was hoping you could give me some pointers on how I can find her a date… or two."

She quirked her brow. "I'm not sure I understand, Mr.

Hilton. You want to find a companion for your mother, but you'd like to do it yourself?"

He didn't like the look in her eyes or her skeptical tone. In business, it was always the first sign of a deal going bad.

"Maybe I should start at the beginning."

He gave her a brief rundown of his parent's thirty-five year marriage and then skipped to these last six months. That was when his mother seemed to have settled with the idea of life after his father, and that his brother's assignment in Afghanistan wasn't a death sentence. She'd gotten past her worries and her mourning and had officially entered the stage of healing called Drive Clint Crazy.

Margot made a number of notes as he spoke, and when he was done, she set the pen down and asked, "Have you suggested your mother get a place of her own?"

"Every time I feel like watching her burst into tears."

She nodded and considered for a moment. "So she doesn't feel capable of living on her own, but *you* feel she's ready for a relationship."

"My mother's capable *and* ready. She's just afraid of being left forgotten and alone. It's unfounded, but unfortunately she's not giving me the chance to prove otherwise. If I were a psychiatrist, I'd say she feels she's lost her husband and youngest son. Sticking at my house is her unconscious way of making sure she doesn't lose me, too. Of course, that's just a guess. I'm not a psychiatrist."

"No, but you'd like to be a matchmaker."

Ouch. He'd walked right into that one.

He studied her for an extra beat and damn, if he didn't sizzle over her no-nonsense style. He liked sharp women who weren't intimidated by him. Thanks to his wealth and reputation as one of the area's premier builders, it wasn't always easy finding them.

He scanned the room, now curious to know if she was single. There weren't any family portraits on the antique tabletop, and her ring finger was bare, but that didn't always mean much.

Had Carmen mentioned anything he'd forgotten?

"What exactly are you hoping to get from me, Mr. Hilton?"

"Clint."

"Okay, Clint."

"Well—for a fee, of course—I'd like advice on how I can find a nice man for my mother."

"I'd be more than happy to meet with your mother."

"Yeah, well…" He scratched the back of his neck. "I would love for you to meet my mother. The problem is, she's a little skeptical when it comes to matchmakers."

"That's not uncommon. I'm sure if she came to the office and we talked—"

"No, that's not going to work."

When she raised a brow, he gave in and told her about Palm Springs and the fight between his mother and Marge. He hadn't wanted to go there, fearing he'd insult Margot's profession, but the more he spoke with her, the more he gathered straight talk would get him farther than charm.

"Unfortunately, I think you're mistaken about what I do here." She slid a glossy brochure across the table. "I'm a dating counselor. And yes, I do bring couples together, but successful matchmaking isn't something that can be summed up in a couple tips. Much of what I do is consultative. I know all my clients very well, and while there are a number of indicators that can make two people likely candidates for each other, I ultimately work off instinct. It's what differentiates my practice from the typical survey-style dating services."

"I didn't mean to diminish your profession."

That pleasant smile returned. "No offense taken. I'm only

saying that if you want my help in finding a man for your mother, I'd need to meet her. Anything short of that would just be things like—" she shrugged "—suggesting she try volunteer work, or maybe join a local garden club or a gym that caters to people her age."

"She's already done that."

"Does she belong to a church or synagogue?"

He shook his head. "It's not that my mother doesn't get out. It's that she's forgotten how to be single. She doesn't know how to act around men so she comes across flippant and disinterested. And I think she's a little scared."

She kept an understanding expression as he explained, and as he talked to her, he began to believe Carmen had been right in sending him here. He liked Margot's style. Not only did she come across confident and capable, there was something approachable about her that kept him at ease, as though he were talking to a good friend.

A good, sexy friend.

"These issues are very normal for people in your mother's situation," she said. "Many of my clients share those same fears."

"Men my mother's age?"

"A good percentage of my clients are in her age group, yes."

Damn, the woman was perfect for him. Carmen was right. Now he only needed to figure a way to make use of her services. He wondered if it was possible to change his mother's mind about matchmakers. But then he remembered her hour-long rant about Marge and realized it wasn't going to happen.

"But keep in mind, I can't help your mother if she isn't ready to date again," Margot pointed out.

"I know my mother would be open to dating if she felt more

confident with herself. She just needs some help. She needs to brush up on her conversation skills, learn to put out the vibe."

Margot blinked. "The vibe?"

"Sure, *the vibe.*" He flashed his favorite half-cocked smile, the one that caught a woman's attention one hundred percent of the time. And when Margot's eyelids fluttered in response, his playful side couldn't help but take the bait.

Holding on to the smile, he lowered his voice and slid his gaze to her lips.

"It's that unspoken body language that says you'd like to get better acquainted. The look that says you're intrigued, that maybe sometime before the night is over you'd like to share a drink…or something."

A heavy swallow slid down her throat and he trailed his eyes lower, down the curve of her neck to the small beaded necklace that hung at her chest. He dotted his gaze over every bead and went on. "It's an art, you know, letting a person know you're attracted without saying a word." He continued down the neckline of her silky white blouse, into the barest hint of cleavage that teased among the ruffles. He lingered there for a pause, letting his mind wander behind the fabric before continuing over her breasts and down her waist. "Some people have mastered it so well they can practically have sex without laying a hand on each other."

Then he turned his gaze back the way he came, and when it reached her face, he could see the flush in her cheeks had deepened.

Evidently, the look that worked one hundred percent of the time still held its streak.

"Well," she said with a husky edge that she tried to cough away, "that's quite a vibe." She reached for the mug at her side and took a sip. "I've got a few clients who could use a look like that."

"And I've got a mother who needs your help. Maybe we could work a trade."

She blinked back to the moment, though her eyes never left his mouth. "I'm sorry, but as I've said I can't do much without meeting your mother."

He glanced down at the brochure in front of him. Margot's list of credentials was long, as were the lengths she went through to make sure her clients were top-notch. She ran background checks, conducted interviews, took references and searched databases he'd never even heard of. Call it instinct. Call it a gut reaction. But he knew without a doubt, Margot was exactly what he needed—someone who understood his mother's situation and would keep her best interest at heart.

"Then we'll have to figure out a way for you to meet her." He leveled his eyes with hers. "Her only problem is with using the services of a matchmaker. She wouldn't have anything against you personally."

"I don't understand."

Clint didn't exactly, either. He was thinking out loud, but the more he thought, the more intent he was to get Margot and his mother together.

"Have dinner with us."

"I won't lie about my profession if that's where you're going."

"The only thing you need to lie about is the fact that I've hired you. We'll tell her you're a friend, or—"

"Mr. Hilton, honesty in relationships is one of my core principles." She flipped the brochure over to show him, and sure enough, there it was right there in big hunter green letters.

"I'm not asking you to date my mother. I'm asking you to get to know her so you can help me find her a man."

She opened her mouth to argue, but he cut her off with his ace in the hole that always got him what he wanted.

"I'll pay you five times your regular fee."

The argument caught in her throat and she sat with her mouth open. "I'm very expensive."

"I'm very intent on getting your help."

She didn't seem to know what to say to that, so he kept going. "It's simple. We're honest about everything. I'm renovating the Fuller building on 6th. Where do you typically have lunch?"

"Capras. It's an Italian deli—"

"I know it well." He folded his hands and continued. "We met at Capras. I asked you to dinner at my place. That's all she has to know."

"I'm not sure…"

She was wavering, but he knew the temptation of money had her considering it. Money always had that effect on people. And to cinch the deal, he went in for the kill.

"Have dinner with me and my mother, once, twice, however many times you need. Be completely up-front and honest about everything, aside from the one little tidbit about me paying you to be there—five times what you usually charge."

"You have no idea how much that is."

He resorted back to the winning smile. "I have a feeling you're worth every penny."

Her eyes fluttered again and he knew he was on the brink of getting his way.

"My standard contract would have to be altered. This is rather unusual—"

"Write it up as you see fit and send it over to my office."

She bit her lip and studied the brochure between them. He knew he nearly had her, and the fact that she was asking questions was good.

"I don't know what guarantee I can offer, with my hands tied, I'm not sure—"

"Guarantee that you'll have dinner with me and my mother for any set number of times you feel is necessary to offer a consultation." Then he met those big brown eyes with his most serious and assuring expression. "That's all I'm asking."

She stared at him for a long time. Long enough for his conscience to question if he truly wanted this for his mother or if there was a teeny little side of him that wanted a date for himself. Not that he'd ever had to pay a woman to date him. But the sentiment remained. This discussion had left him both intrigued by Margot Roth and nearly certain there was something brewing between them. It was the subtle spark of chemistry he'd felt the second he'd stepped into her office. And through this conversation, that spark wouldn't die.

If Margot needed to get to know his mother, Clint suspected half the fun could be getting to know Margot in return. A win-win, so to speak. The virtual golden egg when it came to business dealings. Or business dealings that turned to pleasure.

"I'll do it," she finally said.

Clint smiled and pulled a business card from his wallet. "I think we'll make a good team."

"Maybe I can feel her out. The best solution would be to ultimately warm her up to the idea of using my services. That way, I could offer a standard contract with the standard guarantees. At this point, all I can—"

He rose. "Stop worrying. If I wasn't sure I'd get my money's worth, I wouldn't have made the offer."

Her smile was laced with trepidation, but he had a sense that the next time he saw her—after she'd had a chance to think this through and come up with an action plan—the sharp and confident Margot Roth would make a grand return. In fact, he'd almost bet on it.

When she pushed from her chair, he offered his hand. "Call me when you've got a contract and we can discuss next steps."

MARGOT TOOK THE HAND of the tall, sexy man who had waltzed into her office and turned her afternoon on end. She could tell by his casual ease that this meeting was simply another stop in an average day for Clint Hilton. Rarely did he walk away without closing a deal, she presumed, and she had to admit, he was good. He'd pushed all the right buttons to have her lapping out of his hands. And as he said his goodbyes and made his way out of her office, she felt she'd just witnessed a master at work.

What had she done? For a woman who worked off strict principles, who believed in demonstrating the same ethics she expected of her clients, she'd somehow managed to throw it all out the window by something as basic as money and charm.

But oh, did Clint Hilton have charm. That sexy look alone nearly had her going along before he'd sunk the eight ball by quintupling her salary. She'd practically felt his fingers running all over her as he'd demonstrated "the vibe." Heck, she might have offered her services at half price if he'd done it again, and it amazed her that something so primal could hold so much power.

For someone who thought she knew everything about dating, that look was one for the record books. She lowered back to her chair and reached for her water, wishing it was something stronger.

"And what did tall, rich and handsome want from you?"

Margot looked up to see Alan standing in her doorway. He was a tall, tanned man with a voice smooth as syrup and a calming manner that always put her at ease. Except today, it would take more than her business partner to shake the effects of Clint Hilton from her nerves. And only when she spoke and heard the trembling in her own voice did she realize the ramifications of what she'd done.

"I think I just agreed to be his girlfriend."

4

MARGOT SPENT the bulk of her afternoon drawing up a contract for Clint after consulting with Alan and running the details by her lawyer. Though she could have e-mailed the final document to Clint's office before leaving for the day, she decided to sleep on it instead. Not only did she want to give the ad hoc contract a fresh read-through in the morning, she also didn't want to look too eager in Clint's eyes.

That had been Alan's suggestion, and one of the first things he'd schooled her on when they'd gone into business together five years ago. When it came to people with money, never look like you need their business.

As a military brat who'd grown up entirely middle-class, Margot never once scoffed at Alan's advice on L.A.'s upper crust. And she'd done well for it. She wasn't going to start ignoring him now.

"Well, I'm off to spend a quiet evening with the girls," Alan announced from her doorway. The "girls" were the twin beagles, Lucy and Ethel, that Alan shared with his life partner, Gene.

"Gene's not back from his conference?" she asked.

"No, and it's still raining in Boston. He called this morning to say he was freezing his ass off."

"You didn't tell him about our heat wave, did you?"

Alan chuckled. "He'd already heard. Anyway, I'm off. You'll lock up?"

"Yes, and thanks again for your advice today. It really helped having someone else to brainstorm this contract with."

"I don't suppose it's every day you're contracting yourself out as a fake girlfriend."

She wiggled her eyebrows. "For five times my regular fee."

"Yeah, well, I wouldn't repeat that in too many circles," Alan replied, chuckling. "People will get the wrong impression about what we're selling here at Intimates."

Margot snorted. "I don't think anyone would mistake me for a high-priced hooker. I don't have the legs for it." Then she looked down her chest. "Or the rack."

"I'm sure Rob would disagree."

The mention of her boyfriend doused the smile on her face. "Gosh, Rob, I forgot all about him. I really should call and make sure he doesn't have a problem with this."

"Why would he?"

Margot couldn't think of a reason. She was certain he'd be fine with what, for all intents and purposes, was a few casual business dinners. But she and Rob had barely been dating a month, and with her feelings for him growing stronger by the minute, she didn't want any misunderstandings interfering with their budding relationship.

"I'm sure he won't," she agreed. "But I'll call just the same."

When Alan said his goodbyes and left, she locked the door behind him and made the call.

"Sloan Enterprises," she heard Rob say.

She put on her lowest and most breathy voice. "Hey, sexy."

The line fell silent for an instant before he finally replied, "Margot?"

"Yes, silly. Who else would it be?"

"Uh, I don't know."

"Don't tell me your mother calls you sexy because that

would be kind of weird, and I've already had enough weirdness today."

The befuddled tone in his voice relaxed and he laughed. "Hardly, babe. You're the only one who talks dirty to me."

"You sound distracted. Did I catch you at a bad time?"

"No, not at all. What's up?"

Sitting back in her chair, she kicked off her shoes and told him about her day and the new client she'd taken on. It felt good relaxing like this and reflecting over the day's events with someone like Rob. It reminded her of her parents, how the two had always unwound in the evenings while her mother cooked dinner and her father went through the mail. They were comfortable and easy together. Two partners in the business of running a family and sharing their lives. Margot had always wanted a relationship like that, and had been smart and patient enough to wait for the right man to come along. And when she'd met Rob, she'd known he was the one.

She'd taken notice when they'd met at a charity function the month before. The two had been seated next to each other at a dinner to raise money for the women's shelter where she volunteered and had hit it off before the salads were served. In the span of the two-hour dinner, they'd discovered the same tastes in movies, music, books and sports. They were both raised in similar households, their families traveling often due to Rob's father's career in sales and Margot's life as the daughter of a Marine. They were the middle children in their respective families and shared that special understanding of life stuck between the firstborn and the baby.

It seemed the list went on and on—similar career aspirations, ideas about family and friends, politics and religion. On paper, she and Rob were about as perfect as they came. And in the weeks since that first date, Margot had become almost certain she'd met that ideal life partner she'd been waiting for.

"I think that's great," Rob said when she'd finished her story about Clint.

"So you don't have a problem with me pretending to be another man's girlfriend for the next few weeks?"

"Of course not."

A smile spread across her lips. She loved his faith and trust in her, and it underscored the feeling that she'd found her Mr. Right.

From the time Margot and her friends had entered their teen years, Margot had good instincts when it came to putting men and women together. So much so that by the time she'd graduated high school, she'd known her future was in matchmaking.

Ten years later, she was doing exactly that. She had a solid list of clients and a growing list of success stories. And now that she'd met Rob, she could count herself among them.

"I have to confess, I have reservations about accepting the fee he's offering," she told Rob. "It seems excessive, even for someone who can afford it."

"I disagree. I think what he's paying is just. I mean, think about what you're providing. For one, you're making house calls. And two, he's expecting you to find his mother a date with one hand tied behind your back. That's definitely worth the bump in pay."

She hadn't thought of it that way.

"It's going to be a challenge," she admitted.

"And you'll rise to it, I'm sure. You're very competent, Margot. I think you'll have fun trying to figure out how to hook this woman up without thinking she's using a matchmaker."

Her heart swelled with his assurance. "Thank you."

"You'll do fine. Instead of worrying, you should celebrate your new client."

"That's a great idea. How about we have dinner tonight? You might even coax me into cooking." Which would keep him at her place for who knew what afterward.

"I'd love to, babe, but I've got plans."

She waited for him to elaborate, and when he didn't she resisted the urge to pry. "Well, tomorrow maybe."

"Yeah, give me a call." She heard papers shuffling before he added, "And speaking of plans, I need to take off now, but I'm glad you called. Congratulations. I'm proud of you, babe."

"Thanks."

She wanted to say something more, but she didn't know what, so she opted for a simple goodbye before hanging up the phone. Though her sensible side told her to keep taking things one day at a time, she had to admit a sense of anxiousness when it came to their relationship. She was so sure of their future together, of him being the ideal man for her in every way, she wished they could skip the formalities of dating and go straight to the altar.

Of course, that went against every rational word of caution she handed out to her friends and clients. She'd never felt that rushing a relationship was prudent, and she intended to heed her own advice. But having some permanence and formality between them would certainly be nice, especially when she considered having to deal with men like Clint Hilton.

Clint's musky scent still hung in her office, taking her mind back to their meeting this afternoon. She recalled the silky way his gaze had slid over her when he'd demonstrated the vibe. Remnants of that look still tingled in her insides, calling to her in forbidden temptation. Now that she'd seen the man in action, she didn't doubt all the stories Carmen had told her about him—the womanizing, the playboy vacations in every party spot on the globe. The man had the "It" factor and knew how to use it, which made him dangerous to any woman who didn't watch herself. Margot had to admit that when he'd caressed that smooth gaze over her body, she'd felt naked and unguarded. Even a little aroused. An engagement ring would make a nice safeguard against a man like Clint. Because while Margot had her preferences set firmly in mind, she had no doubt Clint Hilton could turn a woman stupid with the wink of one crystal blue eye.

Blinking away the thought, she gathered her things and shut the lights in the office. While Clint might have touched her lustful side, her good senses reminded her that Rob was her future, and she'd simply keep that in mind as she played this phony courtship.

But as she locked the door behind her and headed for her car, she couldn't shake the feeling that it might be easier said than done.

"TELL ME AGAIN where you met this woman?" Jillian asked as Clint dropped four bags of groceries on the stone counter in his kitchen.

"Capras. It's a deli down on 4th." He stepped over to his wine rack and pulled off two bottles of cabernet.

"Hmm, you don't waste time, I'll give you that. It was barely a week ago that treacherous blonde stormed out of here and you've already found someone new."

He would have moved a lot sooner if work hadn't kept him so busy this week. But now that he considered it, it probably ended up for the better. It would have looked strange suddenly bringing Margot around if he'd just had another date two nights before.

He winked. "Have you ever known me to beat around the bush?"

She gave him a wry smile. "I suppose not."

She began helping him unload groceries, surveying every item in the bags as though she could size up his intentions based on his shopping list. Eyeing a small can of imported caviar that cost nearly as much as the blue sapphires on her ears, she stated, "My, you're putting on quite a spread tonight. Are you sure you want me to stay and join you?"

The comment was made under the guise of a considerate gesture, but Clint knew damn well his mother would hold it against him if he asked her to take a hike for the night. It was a little game they'd been playing for years. She made polite offerings and he had to figure out which ones were sincere. Like the time he'd inadvertently made plans on a Sunday that ended up being Mother's Day. His mother insisted he keep his reservations and swore that it would be perfectly fine to celebrate Mother's Day two days early. So he'd believed her and went on his trip, only to spend the next three years hearing about that one disappointing Mother's Day where she didn't have both sons with her.

That was when Clint discovered that what his mother said and what she expected were two different things.

"Absolutely not. This is your home, and you are joining Margot and me for dinner."

She tried to keep a poker face, but he didn't miss the twinkle of pleasure in her eye.

"Really, it's your first date and you obviously want to impress her." She held up a bottle of finely aged balsamic vinegar. "I'd be a third wheel."

"You'll be pleasant company." Then he shoved a bunch of garlic chives in her hand and asked her to chop them.

Round one; advantage Clint.

For the next hour the two worked together in the kitchen, preparing one of the many meals he'd learned to cook from his father. Cooking had been one of Jerald Hilton's hobbies that had grown out of necessity when he was a young college student at UCLA. Unlike Jillian, who was born into wealth and had staff to take care of the family's basic necessities, Jerald had worked his way to the top. Of course, the rich relations he'd married into hadn't hurt his career, but at his core, Jerry Hilton was part of the working class who took pride in the things he could create with his own hands, a superbly crafted meal being one of them.

"This is nice, cooking with you," Jillian said as she whisked together a vinaigrette for the salads that sat chilling in the fridge. "It reminds me of the early days with your father." Then she looked around his high-tech kitchen. "Although the accommodations are quite a bit better than the tiny apartment we had when we were first married."

The tiny apartment she referred to was the two-thousand-square-foot penthouse three blocks off Wilshire Boulevard her parents had bought the young couple as a wedding present.

"You know, your father cooked a meal like this for me on our first date," she added. "It's how I knew he was serious about me."

She threw him a glance that asked if the same significance applied to Margot.

"I like Margot," he said. "As far as being serious about her, it's a bit premature to say at this point."

The look on her face said she knew he was lying, and that was okay. As long as she didn't know *why* Margot was special, she could think what she wanted. In fact, it was probably best his mother presumed he had serious intentions. She might open up more freely if she thought she was conversing with a future daughter-in-law instead of another one of Clint's casual flings.

And in reality, if it weren't for what he'd heard from Carmen, that might have been true.

Clint had already been impressed with Margot after their meeting, and then the contract she'd drawn up etched another checkmark in her favor. She hadn't missed a beat in the five-page document. Every point had been covered in a manner that was clear and firm, yet fair to both parties. And the fact that she'd whipped it up overnight underscored the fact that his intuitions had been on the mark.

Margot Roth was as sharp as she was sexy, a fact that both intrigued and dismayed him.

Because after returning from her office, he'd made a beeline to Carmen to find out everything he could about the beautiful matchmaker with the big brown eyes. And what he'd learned was that if he wanted more than her business, he'd come around a month late. Apparently, Margot had a boyfriend, and though the relationship was new, Carmen seemed to think it was already serious.

Clint couldn't deny that the news irked him, not so much because she was taken, but because he'd only missed her single status by a few short weeks.

He hated being denied something he wanted, but even more than that, he couldn't shake the inexplicable feeling that she should be *his*. He didn't know where it came from. Hadn't felt that way about a woman before. It was just this *thing* that had come over him and kept sticking like glue. An over-whelming feeling of possession.

It was like walking into a gallery and seeing a painting he knew he had to have. If pressed to articulate why, he'd have a hard time because it wasn't simply the colors, or the style, or the frame or the subject matter. It was the way they all came together in a package that hit that special sequence of buttons.

Except this time, the artwork had a big Sold sign on it.

"Have I seen her in any films?" his mother asked.

"Margot isn't an actress."

"Oh, so she's a model?"

He frowned. "I date women besides models and actresses, Mother."

"Then what *does* she do?"

"I don't know. Some kind of counselor." He followed her onto the terrace, where she proceeded to set the table while he put out the steaks and readied the grill. "We only spoke briefly while we were ordering lunch. I intend to find out the details tonight."

"Well, I'll hand it to you. You don't have trouble finding women, that's for sure."

The doorbell rang and he glanced at his watch to see that she was exactly fashionably seven minutes late. Hell, even her promptness was perfect. As he trekked to the front door, he reminded himself that Margot was here on business, and as much as he would have liked to throw in the pursuit of pleasure, it wasn't worth harming his integrity. His father had always told him that in their business, honor and reputation meant everything, and one's personal life could never be separated from the job. Few people could get away with being unscrupulous in private while still maintaining respect in the business world, and rather than test those waters, it was best to regard all aspects of his life as a piece of the whole. Do right by people, and for the most part, people will do right by you.

In this case, that meant not trying to steal a woman from another guy, no matter how much he might want her.

But as he opened the door and saw Margot standing there in a sexy yellow sundress, her dark coffee eyes bright and dewy and that smile wide and inviting, he couldn't stop one phrase from taunting him.

All's fair in love and war.

5

CLINT OPENED the door wearing flip-flops, tan cargo pants and a Hawaiian shirt, which on further inspection, had barely conspicuous UCLA emblems printed among the palm fronds. It was classic California weekend attire, but coupled with his good looks and perpetual aura of wealth, he looked less like a typical beach bum and more like a guy who'd just spent the weekend kicking back with Jimmy Buffett.

He scanned her over and flashed that million-dollar smile. "You look beautiful."

It was a compliment he'd probably tossed to dozens of women at his door, but she still couldn't help the giddy thrill. As if the cutest boy in class had finally turned his attention to the studious bookworm parked next to the teacher's desk.

She shook it off and reminded herself that this was a business meeting. It would be bad enough having to fake her way through this night; she didn't need to get carried away with the idea this was a real date.

Because when she stepped through the door and into the foyer, she realized how ridiculous that notion was.

She'd been surprised when pulling up to the address. From the front, the house looked like a simple mid-century modern with nice but modest landscaping. But when he opened the door and she crossed the threshold, she realized the facade was only a portal to a level of extravagance she'd never witnessed without having to pay for the tour.

Immediately upon entering, her eye was drawn through a vast great room to the floor-to-ceiling glass walls that showcased a spectacular view of the city. To her right, a soaring stone fireplace made the backdrop for a print that was unmistakably Warhol, and she didn't even want to get a closer look at the Picassoish looking piece that centered the ebony wood dining table.

"I hope you like steak," he said. "Carmen said you weren't a vegetarian."

"No," she replied absently. "Steaks are fine."

She counted three separate seating areas, each adorned with sleek modern furniture that would have made Alan drool. Heywood-Wakefield, Eames, Knoll, all the classics were here as well as the contemporaries responsible for reviving the minimalist, modern style of the 1950s and 1960s. The colors were bright, the layout meticulously arranged so as not to compete with the showcase of the room, which was the view of West Hollywood.

Margot had always had an interest in design and had even taken some courses in college. And though this particular style was far more Alan's taste than her own, she couldn't help but appreciate what she'd walked into—not to mention the amount of money in the room.

She tried not to gawk, knowing that to pass herself off as one of Clint's real dates she'd have to eventually close her mouth and push her eyes back in their sockets. But it was hard. She'd known the man was rich, but even Alan's friends—the bulk of whom came from big money—didn't hold a candle to this.

"Did you have trouble finding the place?" Clint asked.

Her gaze went to an oversized glass mobile that reflected

prisms of colored light onto a stark white wall. "I just followed the cast of *Cribs*."

Clint laughed. "I doubt MTV would be interested in me."

His modesty was cute, but it didn't keep her from feeling insignificant and entirely out of place. Having spent the bulk of her life in military housing, she couldn't imagine living somewhere like this. She doubted she'd ever get past the sensation that some day the real owners would come home from their villa on the Riviera and wonder what the hell she was doing in their house.

And she was expected to pretend she was actually dating this man?

He led her through the room, and when she got closer to the Warhol, she had to ask.

"That's real, isn't it?"

She didn't know how she could tell. Maybe only because it had a different look from the Warhol prints she'd seen at the local poster shops.

He shrugged. "I like art," he said, making her feel even more like a wide-eyed social misfit.

She had the fleeting fear this was all a big mistake. There was no way Clint's mother would believe he'd actually date a woman like her. Not that Margot walked around with an inferiority complex. She was simply a realist. She'd been around L.A. long enough to know that guys like Clint didn't go for regular working girls who barely knew the difference between Gucci and Prada, who wouldn't consider shooting up Botox or shoving silicone in their boobs, and were revolted by the thought of intentionally throwing up a perfectly good meal.

It just didn't happen. Which meant not only did she have to convince his mother to use her services, she had to do it all while selling the notion that she actually belonged in a place like this.

Suddenly, five times her regular fee seemed like a pretty reasonable deal.

"My mom's on the terrace. Come on out and I'll fix you a drink."

He must have noticed that she needed one, and once again, she had to mentally pull herself together. Her father hadn't raised her to freeze up with fear. On the contrary, he'd spent most of her life preaching that in his line of work, fear got you a bullet through the head. He used to say that if a kid could overcome fear in the jungle of Vietnam, she could overcome anything the streets of America could throw at her.

She stood for a moment and imagined him in the room with her, urging her along, even though in reality he was probably in his underwear, tipping back a Budweiser watching *FutureWeapons* reruns on the Military Channel. But still, it calmed her, and she managed to cross the room and step onto the back terrace without ogling anything else.

A beautiful woman who looked barely over fifty rose from a cushy patio sofa and smiled.

"Mom," Clint said. "This is Margot."

"Jillian," the woman said, stepping forward and extending a hand.

She had Clint's eyes, vivid blue and full of life, and her handshake was firm and proper. She wore a blue-and-yellow striped sleeveless button-down over slim white pants cropped at the ankles. A pair of beaded low-heeled sandals balanced the blue studded gems in her ears, and the faintest hint of makeup played up her features without going overboard. The ensemble was summery yet tasteful, conservative with a spot of flair.

In a word: Perfect.

Based strictly on appearances, Jillian Hilton could pretty much take her pick from at least a dozen of Margot's clients, giving Margot the lift to her confidence she needed right now. She had a job to do, and it was time she believed she could do it.

A high-pitched yelp caught her attention, and she looked down to see a caramel-colored ball of fluff with two bright eyes and a shiny black nose. The dog ran to her side and began circling her feet.

"Pom Pom, no!" Jillian scolded.

Clint grabbed Margot's forearm and pulled her toward him. "Watch it. That thing will pee on your shoes."

"She only does that to you because you frighten her," Jillian huffed. "If you weren't so hostile to the poor thing, it wouldn't happen."

Clint pulled Margot closer and held her against his chest as if she needed protection against the two-pound cotton ball. And as he braced her against him, she could have sworn she felt his long inhale at the nape of her neck.

"I'd rather not take the chance," he said.

Jillian grabbed the dog. "I'll go put her in *my room,*" she said, emphasizing the words *my room* and throwing Clint a sideways glance Margot guessed had something behind it.

The woman disappeared into the house, and after one beat too long Clint released his hold and let Margot step away.

She turned and stared at him for a second, nearly asking if that had been a ploy to cop a feel, but then she remembered who he was. Clint Hilton could have any woman he wanted, and from what she'd heard from Carmen, he made use of that benefit as often as possible. The thought that someone like her would catch his eye was ludicrous at best and she kept her mouth shut, thankful she'd stopped to think before she embarrassed herself in front of her new client.

"It was just a little dog."

He moved to the bar and began pouring a glass of red wine.

"That feather duster with legs can wreak more havoc than you know."

She took the wine he offered as Jillian returned to the patio and regarded Margot.

"Oh, you're still here," she said, blinking with obvious surprise.

There was that glance between them again. What was going on with these two?

"Mother," Clint warned.

"Did you expect me to leave?" Margot asked, confused by the statement.

Jillian smiled and returned to her sofa. "Some women haven't appreciated my son's regard for my well-being."

"Margot already knows you live here," Clint said.

"It's been said that how a man will treat his wife can be foretold based on how he treats his mother. You'd think more women would consider that."

Margot took a seat in the adjoining sofa while Clint began fiddling with the grill. "Clint had mentioned that you'd lost your husband a while back. I'm very sorry."

There was no mistaking the look of approval in Jillian's eyes. "Thank you," she said. Then she turned to her son. "Where did you say you two met?"

"The deli, mother."

"That's right. And Clint said you were some sort of counselor."

As if he could make himself more obvious, Clint stopped and stared, holding his eyes on Margot awaiting her answer.

"Yes, I have a practice downtown."

"Is it family counseling, marriage? What area do you specialize in?"

She could feel Clint's stillness as though he were sucking the air from the space. She'd told him she wouldn't lie, and she had no intention of doing so. But he could have a little more faith in her prowess.

"I work with individuals, mostly. Relationship counseling. Singles who have issues that are preventing them from forming relationships. A number of things along those lines." Then she quickly diverted the subject. "I heard you've just joined that new gym down on Sunset."

CLINT EXHALED a breath and went back to setting out the steaks and preparing the appetizers while the two women began chatting. It didn't take him long to confirm that he'd known what he was doing in hiring Margot. With every minute that passed, they seemed to warm up to each other, to the point where he couldn't remember having such a pleasant time with his mom. It definitely hadn't been since Nate had taken off for Afghanistan and left him alone.

That had been a difficult time for the family, and Clint supposed his choice in women hadn't helped the matter with his mother. For most of his adult life, he hadn't felt the need for a serious relationship. He'd been intent on playing the field and enjoying his youth, since he knew how quickly life changed once a man settled down and started a family. He had more than a few friends disappear on him, leaving the nightlife in favor of piano recitals and Little League Baseball. Not that his friends weren't happy or that Clint never wanted that for himself. He simply wasn't in a hurry. And his taste in women reflected that.

It was intentional that he stuck with the types who were fun to be with and completely uninterested in children and family. It made playing the field easier. But having Margot here gave him a sampling of the other side, and to his own surprise, he kinda liked it.

"Where did you grow up?" Jillian asked after they'd seated for dinner and began digging in.

"I was born in Oceanside, but we moved around a lot. My dad was a Marine sergeant, so we spent time all over—North Carolina, Virginia, California—we even spent two years in Okinawa when I was a kid."

"Japan, that must have been interesting," Clint said over a bite of steak.

"I was pretty young. Unfortunately, I barely remember it."

"Your father was a career Marine, no wonder I like you," Jillian said. "We're kindred spirits. My father, the Colonel, served in World War II for the United States Army. Even after he retired from service and started his own company, he ran the household like a barracks."

"Your father was a colonel?" Margot asked, clearly impressed.

Jillian's expression turned smug. "It's a well-kept family secret that Dad never made it past major."

Clint choked on a carrot. "You're kidding!"

Jillian nodded, her face bright with the evil pleasure of giving away the news. And it was news.

His mother giggled over her wine and turned to Margot. "One time I took off to San Francisco to be a flower child."

Margot chuckled and gawked wide-eyed over her dinner. "You were part of the Summer of Love?"

"Oh, heavens no. It was 1971 and I'd missed it by four years. That's how sheltered I was. I didn't even know it was all over by then. But I did it. Right after graduating from high school, I had my driver take me up to San Francisco."

Margot gaped. "You ran away from home in a chauffeured car?"

Jillian nodded. "I was so naive I actually thought he would keep it from my parents. They knew where I was every minute."

Clint sat and listened to his mother's story, wondering

who this woman was and why throughout his entire life he'd never heard any of this before.

His mother, a flower child? She'd always been pinned up so tight, he'd never fathom such a thing. To his mom, wearing open-toed sandals was living on the wild side.

"I drove into town expecting to see people dancing in the parks like I saw on TV, but all I found were a bunch of homeless bums. I was home before the sun set." She put her glass on the table and looked at them both. "And the Colonel never mentioned it once. For years, I thought he never knew, until he commented on it over dinner with Jerald long after we were married." She threw her head back and laughed. "I nearly choked on my sorbet. All that time I'd thought he never knew."

The two women laughed and continued with their meals while Clint sat there in utter dismay.

"You never told me any of this," he said.

Jillian shrugged. "You never asked."

"I had to have asked at some point in my life."

"Clint, you're my child. Children are always wrapped up in themselves."

Now she was making him sound like a cad. "I am not." Though he couldn't ever remember sitting down and really talking to his mother about her life and the things she'd done. But still, that didn't make him self-absorbed. He wasn't self-absorbed.

"What else haven't you told me?" he asked.

She slid Margot a sisterly glance and giggled again like a teen. "Wouldn't *you* like to know?"

Though a side of him felt like the outsider in this conversation, he couldn't muster any offense. Truth was, he loved seeing his mother having fun like this, getting a little tipsy and spilling the family secrets. It was like finding a side of her he hadn't known existed.

He listened to them deep in conversation while studying Margot in the dimming light of the dusky sun. A tiny breeze lifted wisps of her bangs across her face, and she used her slim finger to tuck the wayward strands behind an ear.

He liked her turned-up nose, the way the candlelight shimmered in those chocolate-brown eyes, the way her throat curved delicately down to her chest where those delicious mounds of cleavage fell neatly into her sleeveless sundress.

She'd dressed perfectly tonight. Casually sexy, yet conservative enough for dinner with his mother. And for some reason, he doubted she'd agonized over the ensemble. Instead, she seemed the type to know just the right thing to wear, to say and do, without the drama some women went into.

He loved that confidence she exuded. Not arrogance, by any means. Just a simple comfort in herself and her easy ability to make conversation. Without question, he could see her entertaining clients and associates the way his mother had for his dad all those years. And with a flash of recognition, he felt as though he were witnessing his future.

And damn if he didn't like it.

The two women kept chatting, talking about life as the daughters of military men, moving about the country, though his mother saw the world on vacation while Margot viewed it through the windows of Marine bases. The two didn't exactly grow up on the same side of the fence, but that didn't seem to raise any barriers he could see. Instead, they seemed fascinated by each other's lives, and in turn, Clint grew more intrigued by the enchanting woman he'd invited to dinner.

All's fair in love and war.

That phrase wouldn't stop haunting him, along with the idea of leaving the fast lane behind for a steady future with the right woman. He'd passed thirty last year, and he never had wanted to be one of those pathetic bachelors who didn't recognize when he'd gotten too old for the swinging single life.

For the rest of dinner and well beyond dessert, he held his eyes on Margot, turning sinful ideas over in his head, wondering how hard it would be to pull her away from this guy she was dating and take her for his own. He wanted to test the waters, to see if this draw he felt toward her was in any way two-sided. And so when his mother stood up and announced she was going to retire for the night he didn't try and stop her.

Margot looked at her watch. "Goodness, it's later than I realized." Then she smiled at them both. "I guess it's true that time flies when one's having fun."

His mother wrapped an arm around her new best friend. "Well, I want you and Clint to continue having fun. I'm going to bed, and for your information, my bedroom is on the far side of the house upstairs over the kitchen." She winked. "You don't need to worry about privacy. I'm so tired from the day, I'll be out like a light and you two will have the house to yourselves."

Subtle, Mom.

But he appreciated it just the same. Some time alone with Margot sounded pretty good, and he was suddenly reminded of the fact that he was now in his fourth week of celibacy thanks to his most recent failed date. He was overdue, and he had the perfect prescription standing right there in a sexy yellow sundress.

So when Jillian finally said good-night and left them alone, he didn't waste any time.

Margot had moved to the sink on his terrace where they'd been stacking the dishes all night, and when she'd set their plates down, he came up behind her.

"Amelia will clean this up tomorrow."

His eyes trailed down the silky curve of her back where it dipped behind the flowery fabric. Her zipper hung square and center, egging him to slide it down and drop the pesky dress to the ground.

"Amelia?" She turned to face him, and when she saw how close he stood, her eyes widened just a bit.

"My housekeeper. She'll take care of this." He took Margot's hand in his and brushed a thumb across her knuckles, willing away the urge to press those delicate fingers to his lips for a taste. Instead, he squeezed them gently. "You were wonderful tonight."

She smiled. "I learned a lot about your mother."

"So did I." He took the other hand and held it as well. "And I learned a lot about you, too."

She tried to dismiss it, the touch *and* the comment. "Just doing my job."

"You do it well. I'll bet you've already got a mental list of men that would be perfect for my mother, don't you?"

Her expression said he'd nailed it.

"I'd like a little more time with her before we go there, though," she said.

He dipped his chin to level their eyes. "I think that's an excellent idea. How about dinner tomorrow night?"

She scoffed. "Don't you think that's too soon? Maybe we should be more casual with this. I wouldn't want her to get suspicious."

"Then just have dinner with me."

The look on her face said she hadn't missed where he was going, and to his offense, she tried to back up a step. Clint wasn't exactly accustomed to women backing away from his advances.

"I don't think I understand," she said. But the way she slid her gaze down to his chest said she understood very well.

Her fingers began to tremble in his palms, though the hungry look in her eyes said it wasn't from fear. Clint doubted Margot Roth was afraid of anything, and the fact that she hadn't pulled from his grasp said even more.

"I'm thinking why pretend to date when we could be doing it for real?"

Her gaze shot back to his. "Dating for *real*."

She didn't need to make it sound so absurd.

"I like you, Margot. I like you a lot. And if you tell me right now that you don't feel the same way, I'll back off and leave you alone."

He closed the gap until he felt her breath against his neck. Her lips parted slightly, and it took the strength of twenty mules to keep from kissing her right then.

"I...um...I..."

She couldn't answer, which meant she wasn't saying no. And not being one to sit around and wait, he opted to make the choice for her.

"Time's up," he said. Then he pulled her in his arms and closed his mouth over hers.

6

WHO KNEW A KISS could literally curl a gal's toes? Up until this moment, Margot always thought that was just a figure of speech. But when Clint pulled her into his arms and pressed his lips to hers, that's exactly what happened.

Fireworks. Sparks. Angels singing sweet hymns. Every silly cliché she'd heard from friends and clients became reality, except there wasn't anything silly about it. This was lust in all its pure glory at a level Margot had never felt before.

Clint pulled her closer and groaned as if she were the most delectable thing he'd ever tasted. He slipped his tongue between her teeth and gently prodded, smooth and sensual, hot and deliberate, while his hands coiled around her, igniting places she hadn't thought had the power to turn her on. The base of her spine, the outer edges of her thighs, spots she never would have labeled erogenous zones came to life under the tips of his fingers.

This was a man who knew how to kiss, whose practiced moves had been perfected to hit every right button and stir all the right nerves.

A voice inside her told her she shouldn't be doing this, she shouldn't be standing there wrapped in the arms of this man, but she couldn't find the will to stop. Her heart sang with the feel of his mouth, the strength of his chest against her breasts and the scent of sweat, sex and man. Their tongues danced and their moans hummed in a rhythm of silky pleasure, and all she wanted was for it to go on.

He clasped her hips and pulled her against him, the firm bulge between his legs making an offer she ached to accept. It left her joyful and senseless, powerless to do anything but sink in and enjoy the ride.

He ground against her and drove the kiss deeper, feeding off her and spilling life through her all at the same time. Never before had a simple kiss packed so much sensation, and she mused that this must be how the other half lived. Tall, sexy men who had all the right moves, and the high-fashion women who could take them.

Except Margot wasn't one of those women, and she definitely wasn't the *other half.*

He moved his mouth down her neck, nibbling his way to her ear where he whispered, "I think we should get to know each other a little better."

It was the minuscule break in the moment she needed to put her senses back together. What the heck was she doing letting her client seduce her? It was unethical on so many levels she didn't know where to start.

"I agree," she said, taking in air as she pressed her palms to his chest and nudged away.

Still dizzy, she wiped the wetness from her lips and straightened her dress, backing up a couple of more steps to put some distance between them.

"Uh, I had something slightly more naked in mind," Clint said.

She glanced up to see that he was serious.

"I don't think so."

"Why not?"

He looked so taken aback, it occurred to her she might be

the first woman to ever turn him down—a decision she was still debating.

"First, you're my client," she reminded them both.

"My mother's your client. I'm just the bystander who finds you incredibly sexy and entirely irresistible."

"You're paying me and this is a gross conflict of interest."

He crossed his arms over his chest. "In what way?"

Okay, so he wasn't a client in the classic sense, but the sentiment remained the same. "I simply don't date clients, or the sons of clients who pay me. You must imagine how my reputation would suffer if I started sleeping with the men who sought out my services."

Especially the ones paying five times her regular fee.

He raised an eyebrow and cocked a half smile. "Is that all you can come up with? Because so far I haven't heard anything about you not being attracted."

She opened her mouth to say it, but the words tripped up in her throat. Damn, he had her there, and the smug look on his face said he knew it.

Desperate, she lifted her chin and tried for haughty. "I'm attracted to black forest cake, too, but that doesn't mean I eat it whenever I want."

It only made him laugh. Could she have thought up something less lame?

"I'm glad you find me amusing."

"I find you very amusing. And adorable, and smart, and sexy. Would you like me to go on?"

Yes! "No."

An urge to flee came over her, fueled by her surety that sleeping with Clint was a bad idea and the very strong desire to do it anyway.

"I think I should go," she stated.

That dampened his humor. He stepped in and clasped a

hand to her shoulder. "Okay," he said. "No pressure." Then his gaze settled on her face. "But I thought that kiss was pretty spectacular. Didn't you?"

She willed herself to say anything but the truth, knowing this wasn't a man to be encouraged. Unfortunately, she'd always been a terrible liar. So much so that she'd nearly sworn off the practice entirely.

"It was pretty spectacular," she admitted.

He laughed again. "Try not to make that sound like such a bad thing."

"It's not. It's just that…" She searched for the words, wishing he'd take his hands off her so she had a shot at thinking clearly. "This is all very surprising. I'm confused and need to think this through."

He conceded by bending in and pressing his gentle lips to her forehead. "I don't want you confused. I want you hot and ready and anxious to go to all the places I'd love to take you."

Then he caressed his palms over her arms and took her hands in his. She watched as he brought her fingers to his mouth and kissed them, all the while holding her gaze with a sizzling look of desire that nearly dropped her to her knees.

She'd never been in the company of a man so versed in seduction, so casually comfortable with himself and so effortlessly at ease in telling a woman exactly the right thing. Even Rob—

She gasped and whipped her hands away.

"I have a boyfriend!" she announced.

He reacted with amusement. "You just thought of that now? My, that's some boyfriend."

Her cheeks flushed. This was horrible. How could she have forgotten Rob? And this was twice in four days—both times in the presence of this man.

"I need to go," she said. Then she turned to fetch her purse.

For the first time since she'd met him he actually sounded unsettled. "I'm sorry, Margot. Don't rush out like this."

She stopped and turned.

"I gave you the hard sell and I apologize," he said. "I don't want to scare you away. This is important for me and my mother."

Her nerves eased and she took a long breath. To be honest, the contract was important to her, too. She'd sunk all her savings into her new condo and this job was the security net that helped her sleep at night. She didn't want to lose it.

"Let's get together in a couple days," she agreed.

He smiled with relief and led her to the door. "Deal."

And just when she crossed the driveway thinking the incident would be left behind them, he called from the doorway, "Besides, we've got plenty of time to deal with the other thing."

"I KEEP ATTRACTING the wrong kind of men."

Margot sat behind her desk and mulled over her latest client. Stacy was twenty-four and worked as a cocktail waitress for Surf's Up, a local meat market for the college-age crowd. That would be clue number one to the cause of Stacy's complaint. Clue number two was her appearance.

The fishnet shirt barely distorted the view of her black satin bra, and if her skirt were any shorter it could be classified as a belt. She wore far too much makeup, an overabundance of jewelry and so much hair spray Margot feared she might be flammable.

Then there was the matter of the strange tinge to her skin. It was tanning booth on overload in an unnaturally dark shade, given her pale features. As if she'd been going for California sun-kissed but had bumped the switch to radioactive.

Margot didn't need to ask, but experience taught her never to presume.

"What kind of men do you attract?"

"Jerks after nothing but sex. The last one didn't even buy me dinner. How's that for a royal scumbag?" She crossed her legs and Margot couldn't avoid a glimpse of hot pink underwear. "That's when I called you. I am *so* done with walking boners. I need a nice guy, preferably one with a job. You can get me one of those, right? That's what you do, isn't it? You're a man broker?"

Man broker. That was a new one.

"Not exactly, but I do have clients who are nice guys with jobs."

Stacy beamed. "Sign me up!"

Margot sighed and pushed back in her chair. Stacy wasn't the first to come in thinking she was running some kind of singles store, as if there were a back room filled with aisles of men to choose from.

This was the place in the interview where she usually lost most of those types of clients.

"It's not that easy," Margot explained. "First, we need to get at why you're attracting the type of men you do."

When her eyes inadvertently dropped to Stacy's chest, the woman shot out, "I need a boob job, don't I? My friends say I'm too flat, that all the good men like them bigger."

Unless Stacy's friends were plastic surgeons or owned Hooters, Margot couldn't fathom why anyone would say that. Stacy had a perfectly adequate pair of C cups. In fact, she had a lot of wonderful things going for her. It was just a matter of getting the right ones in the forefront and leaving the rest to the imagination.

"Your breasts are fine," she assured. "But your clothing is a different story."

Stacy blanched, as if that was the last thing she expected to hear.

"Is this how you dress all the time?" Margot asked.

"Of course. If I didn't, no one would look at me at all!"

"You'd be surprised how many men would still approach you if you didn't show so much skin. And they'd be the nicer ones you're looking for."

Stacy eyed her ensemble as if Margot were suggesting she torch her best friend.

"Stacy, the way people dress makes a statement, and your statement is, 'I'm cheap and easy.' You need to cover up some of the goods, tone down the makeup—"

Stacy shook her head. "Oh, no. My eyes are tiny and I've got lizard lips. I look absolutely horrid without makeup."

"—and you're spending way too much time in tanning booths."

"To keep from looking like a ghost!" She held out her arms. "This isn't even a real tan. I can't tan. I've got to paint it on, my skin is that fair."

"And there are nice guys out there who would love a fair-skinned pretty blonde with beautiful green eyes and a gorgeous figure. You aren't going to find the right man—one who loves and respects you—until you are ready to show the world who you really are."

Stacy sat back and considered Margot's words. "I don't know. I had zero love life until my friends made me over."

"When was that?"

Stacy shrugged. "I don't know, high school, I guess."

Margot raised a brow. "Don't you think it's time for a new makeover?"

"Well…maybe."

"You're still dressed like a high schooler, which is why you're attracting the social equivalent of horny teenage boys. You're in your twenties now. It's time to take a step up from that."

"And maybe I'd find men who are better in bed." Stacy tapped a hot-pink fingernail on the profile she'd filled out. "I said on the form that sex is really important to me. Seriously. I can't date any duds."

Sure, I keep the sex gods on aisle five across from the accountants.

Margot held back a groan. "You need to get realistic about your expectations. I won't be trying to find you a man who's great in bed. I'll be looking for a man who complements you on a personal level, who you feel comfortable communicating with, who shares common interests, has the same feelings toward family and friends. When you have that right combination, you'll end up with a sex life that works over the long haul. It may not start out great the first time, but if you're with someone who's willing to explore and who you can communicate with in a positive way, you'll end up with something far better than a hot fire that fizzles out before the third date."

And Margot couldn't help but listen to her own words.

She'd barely slept last night, still reverberating from the sizzling effects of that kiss by Clint. That was definitely the kind of hot fire her client was looking for, but Margot had to heed her own advice.

Sex like that died fast if it wasn't built on a foundation of friendship, respect, honest communication and common ground. Those were the four core principles she preached every day, and without them all one had was hot sex—fun for a while, but quickly turning old and tired if there was nothing else there.

Margot knew without a doubt sex with Clint would be more than satisfying, but as she'd reminded herself last night, she was at a point in her life where she wanted more than that—and she'd found it in Rob. She needed to remember that while she and Rob's sex life hadn't started out with that magical bang, the core principles were there. At this point, the amazing sex she knew they were capable of was only a matter of experimentation.

Experimentation she and Rob were overdue for.

"So you're telling me I could end up with a really nice guy who's lousy in bed, and it's my job to fix him?"

Margot blinked. "I don't know that I'd put it that way. I'm only saying don't make sex such a high priority. Look at the man first. Find someone you really connect with outside the bedroom. And if, when you do make love, it's not everything you'd wanted, communicate what turns you on. Remember, this is for life, not just for now. Even the best sex lives go through lulls and peaks and valleys. Like every other part of a relationship, it's something you have to work at, and if you have the right partner, you can create fireworks and stars."

"You really believe that? I mean, what about chemistry?"

"There's sexual chemistry and there's spiritual chemistry. Find the spiritual one, and you can make the sexual one happen."

Stacy took a long breath and sighed. "This sounds really complicated."

"It's not. You just need to keep what's important firmly in mind and have the strength to let the other stuff go."

Words Margot seriously needed to remember. She knew this lust over Clint was only because she hadn't seen her boyfriend in nearly a week. They'd both been tied up lately, her with work and Rob studying for the actuarial exams he had to take for his job. Life had gotten in the way and their sex life had suffered, making her vulnerable to the temptations of hot, vibrant studs like Clint Hilton.

Margot had to admit she'd had better sex than Rob, but she

never once doubted they could make it the best. They just needed to put some effort into it. And as if this meeting with Stacy had been divine intervention, she realized that's exactly what she needed to do.

She gave Stacy a list of changes to make and then scheduled a follow-up meeting. And when Stacy left, she went to work planning the perfect seduction for the man she should be paying attention to. Rob said he'd had to study tonight, but Margot suspected that if she showed up at his house naked, she might coerce him into taking a break. It was exactly the type of thing she'd been meaning to try and simply hadn't gotten to. But given the recent temptation of her new client, she couldn't think of a better time to put more steam behind her and Rob's sex life.

And a little pink raincoat with matching high heels sounded like just the ticket.

With the rest of her afternoon clear, she ducked out for the night and began making arrangements. She'd cook Rob a nice dinner. He'd marveled over her homemade marinara sauce, and she figured she had enough time to make up a batch before the dinner hour. Some pasta, bread, maybe a little salad could be easily wrapped up in a picnic basket. A hot meal for a hungry soul who'd probably been living off fast food for the last week, the poor guy. She'd heard those actuarial exams were brutal, and was certain he'd appreciate the dinner break.

If not, he'd certainly appreciate what she had in mind for dessert.

With a new spring in her step, she knew this was exactly what she needed—her and Rob alone for some serious sexcapades. And in the process, she'd prove that the right man could stoke a hotter fire than all the hotshot playboys in Hollywood.

7

CLINT STEPPED into the elevator at his downtown office after having spent the bulk of the day in a grueling budget meeting with his latest clients. Mr. and Mrs. Proctor were a wealthy East Coast couple whose Malibu vacation home had burned down in a wildfire, and Clint's company had won the contract to rebuild it. It was a job H & H Associates never would have taken if Clint's father were still alive. Jerry Hilton would have steered clear of the old and stingy blue bloods, saying that some people were more trouble than their money was worth.

Over the years, H & H had passed on a number of jobs because Clint's father hadn't liked something about the prospective clients. And when he died, Clint had thought that widening their clientele would be the legacy he added to the business.

Instead, he'd learned that his dad had been right.

When he should have spent the day scoping out new projects, he'd blown the afternoon having to go over the cost of every last doorknob in the beach house, explaining California building code that included earthquake retrofitting the Proctors didn't deal with in Connecticut. He'd been forced to compromise the quality of construction because Mr. Proctor liked to do his own research, tracking down testimonials to prove that cheaper materials were just as good as standard grade.

And Clint could forget entirely the innovations in green construction the company prided itself on. Apparently, Mr. Proctor's circle of friends didn't believe in global warming, and the childless couple's sour view of the younger generation kept them from caring what shape they left the planet in when they ultimately checked out.

The whole project was turning into a nightmare, and Clint could only wonder if his dad was currently up in heaven shaking his head and saying, "I told you so."

He supposed it was a lesson he'd had to learn on his own, and he'd learned it well.

When the elevator doors opened, he crossed the lobby to his suite, glancing through the glass doors to see Carmen at her desk with a gangly young teenager hanging over her shoulder. The two were looking at something on her computer, and Clint wondered if Carmen knew the kid was currently copping a view of her tits down the front of her starched white shirt.

Clint stepped in, sounding the bell that caught their attention, and reluctantly, the kid ripped his gaze from the cleavage to see who'd joined them.

"Hey, boss man!" Carmen said. But when she caught the look in Clint's eyes, the smile slid from her face. "The meeting was that bad, huh?"

"Worse." Clint gave the kid an assessing glare. "Who's our friend?"

The boy backed from Carmen's chair. "Brad Mahoney."

The name sounded vaguely familiar.

"Edward Mahoney's grandson," Carmen assisted. "You agreed to let him intern this summer."

It came back to him now. Ed Mahoney, one of his father's good friends and their company's most valuable investors, had asked if his grandson could learn the ropes of the contracting business at their firm. Clint didn't usually take on interns, but when asked by business associates with perpetually open checkbooks, it was hard to say no.

"School's out already? It's barely May," Clint asked.

"Yeah, well, uh, I dropped a couple classes that weren't working for me so I'm done early this year."

Clint stared at the kid, wondering what that meant exactly, then decided he didn't want to know.

"I'd scheduled him last-minute not realizing your meeting would go so far over," Carmen explained, her eyes filled with apology. "I'm trying to arrange for him to meet up with Stan, but he hasn't returned my call."

Stan was the company's on-site manager and Clint's right-hand man. Where Clint swung the deals and kept the banks and investors happy, Stan made sure they actually got the job done.

"He stopped by the Fuller job after our meeting," Clint said. "He'll be back in a while."

Brad hitched against Carmen's desk as though he owned the place, and it struck a raw nerve with Clint. Maybe it was the resonating headache from the meeting this afternoon, or his general annoyance at having to take the kid on. But as Ed Mahoney's grandson, Clint had expected someone a little more pulled together.

Brad's dark hair hung haphazardly into blue eyes that had a sleepy quality to them, as if he hadn't quite recovered from last night's beer fest. He'd managed to throw on a dress shirt, though the effort was diminished by the fact that he hadn't tucked it in. And the jeans most definitely wouldn't have been Clint's choice for a first meeting with the boss.

Then again, Clint reminded himself that he'd been green out of college once, that his fuse was currently short thanks to four torturous hours with the Proctors, and that he should probably cut the kid a break. He was on edge, not to mention dead tired, and it wasn't all thanks to the Proctor meeting.

Also to blame was a certain brown-eyed matchmaker and the sizzling kiss that had left him wide-awake half the night.

Clint couldn't remember the last time a woman had left him rapt to the point of distraction. It was basically never. And into the wee hours of the morning, he'd laid in his big and empty bed trying to figure out what to do about it. He'd spent half the night trying to tell himself she had a boyfriend and to get over it and move on, but the gnawing yearning in his gut chose not to listen. And if a night of tousled sleep hadn't shaken it off, it hadn't dissolved in daylight, either.

So he'd spent his day trying to plan his next move while going about the motions—the four-hour meeting not helping the matter any.

Dragging in a long breath, he waved Brad back to his office. "Come with me."

"Whoa! You surf?" Brad asked, gawking at a photo on Clint's credenza as they stepped into his office.

"Not well, but I manage."

Brad picked it up. "What kind of board is that, a Walden?"

Clint shrugged. "Just one I borrowed from the guy I was visiting."

"Dude, that water's crystal. Where was this, New Z?"

When Clint told him Australia the kid went into a lengthy monologue about his wakeboarding in Mendocino, skiing in Sun Valley and the specialty skateboard his mom bought him for Christmas. Clint considered the conversation a decent distraction while he straightened his desk and looked over the mail Carmen had left him.

"That's totally dope. The boss man surfs," Brad concluded. He set the photo on the coffee table instead of the credenza where he found it, then plopped down on the couch and put his feet up as if he were kicking back to watch the Lakers game.

Clint wanted to brush off his annoyance, but the task kept growing harder.

"What are you studying at school, Brad?"

"This and that. Business mostly, and general ed. I'm not crazy about school, but the chicks are hot. They're what keep me from blowing it off, you know what I mean?" He shrugged. "Well, that and my mom would kill me."

"So what exactly are your career plans?"

"Right now my mom wants me to learn about building homes. That might be kinda cool."

"What do *you* want?"

There went another shrug. "I haven't given it much thought."

Clint tried to imagine ever being like Brad, but couldn't. There was never a time he or his brother didn't have their lives figured out. For as long as he could remember, he'd wanted to work with his father, and Nate wanted to be a writer. Maybe it had been the Colonel drumming the importance of planning into their heads when they were kids. Maybe it was his father's love for building things that had rubbed off on him from the start. Most likely it had been a little of both. But no matter what, Clint had never been as vacant of ambition as this kid, and wondered what the hell he was going to do with him for the summer.

Brad waved a hand around Clint's office. "I could go for this. A blingin' office, a hot babe up front. I'll bet you've got some dopin' cars, huh?"

"It took a lot of hard work to get it. Are you up for some work?"

"Sure, I can run with that. Just tell me where to start, boss man."

Clint frowned. "Listen, Brad, you're welcome to call me Clint, but boss man is something only Carmen gets away with."

Brad looked taken aback. "Oh, uh, sorry." Then some sort of realization came over him that had him nodding, winking, and making little pistol gestures with his fingers. "I'm totally there, man."

It came off so odd, Clint had to ask, "Totally where, Brad?"

"You and Carmen." He winked again. "I'm cool with that."

"Cool with what?"

Brad lowered his voice. "The boss-secretary thing. You know, special favors, pet names. I get it. I can be cool."

Clint got it, too, and he wasn't cool.

He stood and leaned on his desk. "Carmen's my office manager, not my secretary, and what we're talking about here is that she's worked for me for four years and you've been here fifteen minutes. And as for special favors, you can do me one right now by pulling your mind out of your jeans and remembering this is a business and not a frat house."

His biting tone wiped the stupid grin from Brad's face. "Yeah, sure."

Clint gripped his forehead and remembered he hadn't taken the aspirin he'd been aching for ever since he left the Proctors' penthouse suite up in Beverly Hills. The headache was now speeding toward a migraine and he was one more *cool dude* from throwing this kid out on his ass.

Then he recalled all the favors Ed had done for them over the years and realized he was screwed. Brad wasn't going anywhere soon, not as long as he kept showing up. And as long as he did, Clint had an obligation to try to teach him something.

He lowered back in his chair and sighed.

"You'll start here at eight o'clock sharp."

"That early?"

When Clint looked the kid in the eye, Brad quickly retorted, "No problem. Eight o'clock."

"Wear jeans and an old T-shirt. And get yourself a pair of steel-toed work boots. You'll be spending most of your time on the job sites."

"Is there, um, an allowance for that?"

Clint's eyes widened. "Yes, it's called a paycheck. You'll get it at the end of the month."

Brad scratched his shoulder. "Okay. But before I forget, next Thursday I've got some things to do. I can probably come in, but it won't be until—"

Oh, for criminy sakes. "Work that out with Carmen."

"Sure, I was just…I figured you'd want to know."

"That's it for today. Take off and get some sleep. You'll need it."

Reluctantly, and looking somewhat confused, Brad rose from the couch and tripped out the door, leaving Clint peacefully alone. He leaned back, closed his eyes and took a long, relaxing breath. Given the crap level of this day, he should really just go home, but that option felt dull and lonely. What he really wanted to do was pick up where he and Margot had left off last night, or at least give it another try.

Glancing at the message light on his phone, he grabbed the receiver and retrieved his voice mail. He'd called her on his way back from the meeting but she hadn't called him back. And after checking the messages on his office phone, she hadn't called him there, either.

He was just setting the phone back down when Carmen stepped in.

"So, what do you think of our new intern?" she asked, a wide grin across her face saying she already had his answer.

"The kid's a post. Next time I agree to take on a rich relation, make sure I've met him first."

She chuckled and set a file on his desk.

"Have we heard from Margot today?" he asked.

"No, should I have?"

He studied the look on her face, trying to tell if she was just playing dumb. After all, she and Margot were friends, and he had made a pass at her last night. Didn't women gossip about stuff like that?

"I left a message this afternoon. I was hoping to get with her and strategize our next move."

"I'm sure she just had a full schedule today. You tried her cell?"

He nodded. "She was either on it or had it turned off. It went straight to voice mail."

"Well, I could try her at home if you'd like."

Now, there was plan. A plan he liked a lot, especially if it came with a slight twist.

"Maybe I'll just swing by her place on my way home," he suggested. "Where did you say her condo was?"

"Not anywhere near your way home." She crossed her arms over her chest and raised a brow. "What are you up to, boss man?"

He feigned ignorance. "Nothing. This is simply important to me. Last night went very well. We've got a good momentum going and I don't want to lose it."

"And this momentum can't wait until tomorrow?"

No, actually, it couldn't. If Clint had walked away with anything last night, it was the certainty that something hot sizzled between him and Margot, and he wasn't about to throw himself out of the ring after only one round. Considering he knew he'd only spend his evening thinking about her anyway, he might as well do it in her company where he had a fighting chance.

He cracked his special smile loaded with the additional

dose of "pretty please," and a half hour later he was cutting out for the day with Margot's address in his hand.

Margot made one last pass over her makeup in the rearview mirror of her Volkswagen Beetle before grabbing her picnic basket and heading up to Rob's apartment. She'd gotten a strange look from her neighbor, Mr. Hanson, when she'd stepped into the front courtyard of her condo wearing her thigh-high bubblegum-pink raincoat and matching leather pumps.

And nothing else.

Of course, Mr. Hanson hadn't known that underneath the light jacket she sported a meager pearl-white thong and satin bustier. Nor was he aware of the fact that inside the basket she'd tucked a stash of condoms between the jar of homemade marinara and a loaf of French bread. But to look at her, any bystander would know she was headed for a very *interesting* evening, one that even her seventy-four-year-old neighbor hadn't missed.

She'd waved coyly and whipped out to her car before he could corner her with questions. It had felt fun and thrilling to do something a little racy and spontaneous. To Margot's friends and family, she was always the sensible one, the proverbial designated driver on the highway of life. She always thought before acting, asked before taking, and from an early age, staked a claim as the perpetual go-to person when someone needed a voice of reason.

So to go prancing out of the house half-naked à la Little Red Riding Hood was definitely out of character. But it was good therapy stepping out of her comfort zone for something daring like surprising Rob with dinner in a barely-there set of lingerie. It got her blood pumping and her heart beating anticipating the look on his face when he opened the door and saw what she'd brought him.

It was the thought that put a grin on her face as she skipped up the stairs to Rob's second-floor apartment.

They'd been dating over a month and had built a good foundation on the four core principles Margot believed in—friendship, respect, honest communication and common ground. Now, with the basics in place, this was exactly the thing she needed to take their relationship and throw it into overdrive.

Adjusting her coat and tightening the belt around her waist, she took a quick breath before rapping on the door. She tried to hold her smile to something smooth and sultry, but when she heard the quick steps approaching the door, excitement bubbled it up to a fat wide grin.

The dead bolt clicked, the knob turned, and when the door swung open, the brassy smile froze on Margot's face. Standing in the threshold was a skinny blonde with bright blue eyes and oversized breasts wearing a tiny tank top and…were those Rob's pajama bottoms?

Margot took in the sight, her thoughts rushing past too quickly to snatch on to any one thing, while the woman looked her up and down.

"You aren't the pizza guy," the blonde said.

Margot settled on the woman's toes. The nails were painted a bright royal blue and a silver ring circled the middle one on the left. They barely peeked out from under the pants she was now certain were Rob's. She remembered commenting on that tear up the right ankle, had made a mental note to buy him some new ones when his birthday came around in July.

This woman isn't having sex with your boyfriend.

In fact, Margot had thought new pajama bottoms would be a highly appropriate gift given the stage of their relationship. Not too expensive, personal but not overdone.

She's not having sex with Rob.

She scaled her eyes up the woman's form, across slim hips and an even smaller waist to disproportionately large breasts.

Stacy's comment came back to her. *All the good men like them bigger.*

Rob wasn't in that class. He was better than that. And this wasn't happening. She was sure of it. There was a misunder-standing buried here somewhere. She just needed to focus, get her mind to work clearly, stop assuming the worst and—

"Are you looking for Rob?" the woman asked.

Margot swallowed and forced herself to speak. "Yes. Is he here?"

Say no. Say he's out of town. You're house-sitting. His brother's girlfriend—

The woman swept her eyes over Margot one more time before replying, "Hold on a sec."

She stepped out of sight.

"Rob, there's someone at the door."

Through the open door, Margot could hear the low voices.

"Who is it?"

"Some broad in a pink raincoat."

"What does she want?"

Margot closed her eyes and searched desperately for air.

"How the hell do I know? Maybe she's a neighbor. Maybe she's locked out or needs to borrow something."

The overpowering urge to turn and run had her moving back a step, but she held fast and willed the courage to stay. She couldn't cut out like this and spend the night assuming the worst. There could be a very logical explanation. This could all simply be—

But when she caught the look on Rob's face as he stepped to the door, every good explanation vanished.

"Margot."

He looked surprised, somewhat guilty and...*was that actually annoyance?*

"You should have called," he said.

"It was a—" she stopped before saying the word *surprise.* Her lunch crept north and she gagged. Reality had sunk in, but her reaction to it was only just now beginning to register.

"Um," he said, holding a beer in one hand and rubbing his forehead with the other. "This is awkward."

"You were studying tonight."

"I am," he started, then realized it was pointless. "Margot, I should have called you last week."

Last week?

He stepped into the hall and closed the door behind him. "I'm sorry. Had I known you'd show up like this, I—"

His eyes slipped over her and she clutched the jacket at her chest. This was, without a doubt, the most humiliating moment of her life.

"I just," he went on. "It wasn't going to work for us."

"Why not?" she choked out, though why she was even still standing there, she didn't know. Maybe it was shock, or the need for answers, or the need to confirm deep down that this was all really happening.

Her boyfriend, the man who had been perfect for her in every way, was not only ending their relationship, he'd already moved on without telling her.

Her throat tightened.

Do...not...cry.

"I like you, Margot. I really do. But the—" He waved a hand between them as he searched for the word. "The *zing* isn't there."

"The zing?"

"You know." Words failed him and he let out an exasperated huff. "When I'm with you, it's like I'm sleeping with my sister."

"You've slept with your sister?"

He winced and shook his head. "You and I make great friends, is what I mean. You're fun and I enjoy talking to you, but when it comes to anything physical, I…I—"

She held up a hand. She'd heard enough. It was already mortifying standing there half-naked holding a picnic basket of condoms, she couldn't take hearing that having sex with her was akin to incest.

He nervously eyed the door. "Look, let's meet for coffee tomorrow. We can sit and talk and I can do a better job of all this."

"That's not necessary."

With her worst thoughts confirmed, her questions answered and all doubt removed, all the things that had been holding her at his doorstep vanished. With only enough control to keep from stumbling down the stairs, she turned and fled like a humiliated, wounded coward. When she should have broken the basket over his head, called him every version of sleazebag in the book and then kicked him in the groin for good measure, all she could do was flee while fighting back tears.

How could this have happened to her? She was the smart one. She was the counselor who made the right choices and saw relationships more clearly than everyone else. She knew the signs and spotted them before everyone else did.

How could she have gotten this so wrong?

"Margot, please," she heard him call behind her. "I don't want us to end like this. Let's talk tomorrow when—"

But she didn't hear the rest. The instant her feet hit the sidewalk, she tore around the corner of the building toward her car, snatched the keys from her pocket, jumped inside and let the waterworks flow.

8

MARGOT PULLED into the carport of her condo and shut off the engine. She hoped since she'd left Mr. Hanson had finished sweeping his front walkway and had retired inside. If the man had looked at her quizzically when she'd walked out of her condo, he'd definitely have questions if he saw her come back so quickly, the bubbly smile on her face replaced by tear-streaked cheeks and puffy eyes.

She pulled a napkin from her glove compartment and tried to dab away some of the damage, but the reflection staring back at her only made her feel worse.

How could she have gotten Rob so wrong?

That was the question that kept playing over in her mind like some bad repetitive lyric that wouldn't end.

Why hadn't she seen this coming? How could she have been so sure about someone who was so obviously not right for her?

This wasn't just about a broken heart. This was her career, a career she'd built on instincts. It was about her four core principles, her virtual key to unlocking the secret to successful relationships.

She'd had all of it with Rob, and what she'd gotten was a giant wake-up call that everything she believed in was incorrect, everything she counted on could fail. It left her feeling raw and unsteady, her confidence in her future and her profession now wobbling on shaky ground.

How could she assume to know what was best for other people if she couldn't even pick the right guy for herself? Up until now, she'd always been in control. Margot Roth didn't make mistakes, much less those relating to men. She was the professional. She was the expert.

So how could she have ended up dumped and alone, thrown out in exchange for a blondie, pizza and beer?

The image brought the tears back to her eyes and she scolded herself—she needed to get out of the car and this ridiculous outfit before she drove herself mad.

What she wanted was a hot bath and a pint of Ben & Jerry's—the best prescription for a woman intent on wallowing in self-pity for at least a day or two.

Stepping from the car, she eyed the long walkway, pleased to see no sign of Mr. Hanson. Now, unless he happened to be hanging out at his front door, she had a chance at sneaking in unnoticed. So grabbing her basket and clutching the mascara-stained napkin at her chest, she rushed down the pathway, rounded the corner and slammed straight into her newest and wealthiest client.

Clint Hilton.

"Wha—?"

Out of reflex, he grabbed her forearms to keep them both from tumbling backward.

"Margot."

She blinked, looked into those sparkling blue eyes, and when they darkened with concern, a flush came over her that had her shrinking in his arms. Oh, God, how much more embarrassing could this day get?

Catching her balance, she clutched the lapel of her raincoat and diverted her gaze. "What are you doing here?"

"I was—are you okay?"

"No, this isn't a good time." She reached for her keys.

"You've been crying. Has something happened?"

"Just a plan gone bad, that's all." He stood between her and her door, and she motioned to get around him. "Do you mind?"

"Oh, sure." He let her pass, but when he followed her to her door she wondered what part of *now is not a good time* he didn't understand. She had no idea what he was doing here, and had no interest in finding out. Not in this ridiculous getup and her makeup cried off her face.

"If you'd call my office, I'd be happy to meet some other time," she tried again.

"Actually, what I wanted to talk about can wait."

Turning the key in her lock, she opened the door. "Good, then I'll talk to you later."

She'd barely made it through the threshold when he braced a hand to the door and followed her inside. "Looks to me like you could use a friend now." He grabbed the basket from her hand, the one filled with dinner and condoms, and brushed past her. "Let me help you with this."

Before she could utter an objection he stepped into her living room, set the basket on the coffee table, then walked back, closed her door and moved to take her coat.

"No!" she yelped, using both hands now to clutch the neckline up to her throat.

He backed away and held his hands up. "No problem. It's just…" He looked her up and down. "A little warm for London Fog." Then his eyes twinkled as he looked her over a second time. "Unless…" A knowing smile popped the dimples in his cheeks. "What exactly was this plan of yours that went bad?"

The heat in her cheeks turned to flames and she knew without a doubt every inch of her skin matched the bright pink tint of her jacket.

"What do you want, Clint?"

"Are you *naked* under there?"

Now the only parts of her body still pale were the white knuckles clenched to her coat.

"That's not your business."

He rubbed a hand to his chin. "You *are* naked under there, aren't you?"

She didn't like the calculation in his eyes, or the fiery intrigue that seemed to be growing with every second.

"What are you doing here?" she asked, her voice becoming strangled.

"At the moment, I'm trying to figure out why a beautiful woman wearing nothing but a sexy trench coat and a pair of killer heels has come home crying."

A lump collected in her throat. She could have held on to her irritability if he hadn't called her beautiful. And sexy. He'd said her trench coat was sexy. It was the reaction she was supposed to have gotten from Rob, but instead, the man had only looked at her like…like…

She opened her mouth to say something but the only sound that came out was a wail. The floodgates opened, tears spilled from her eyes and the death grip she'd placed around her collar collapsed under the weight of the situation.

"Fine, all right," she cried. "My boyfriend dumped me." And to her own horror, she found herself adding, "For a pixie little blonde with big boobs and *blue toes.*"

"Really?" He had the audacity to look pleased which only fed the men-are-pigs opinion she was currently harboring. It was bad enough humiliating herself in front of her client, but she'd obviously also made the mistake of assuming he might possibly understand.

But how could he? He was Clint Hilton. One of West Hollywood's favorite playboys. Rejection wasn't in his dictionary, and humiliation would be about as foreign to him as tacos in Beijing.

Her sobs deepened and he quickly saw the error in his ways. He dropped the thrill from his eyes and pulled her into his arms. "I mean, I'm sorry, hon. That's…horrible."

He held her close and patted the back of her head, making shushing sounds and rocking her in a way she found oddly calming. Though it could have been his aftershave, a scent that mixed rustic earth and fresh sunshine into a soothing blend of aromatherapy. Or the strength of his arms in contrast with the gentle press of his fingers that made her feel both safe and comforted all at once. Or maybe it was the quiet hum of his voice that vibrated against her temples and eased the ache in her head.

Whatever the combination, she found her sobs subsiding and the tension along her spine relaxing. And as they did, the true mortification of the scene seeped in.

Her best client, the man entrusting her to find a companion for his mother, the man paying her an exorbitant amount of money for her services, had just caught her when she was at her weakest and most unprofessional moment.

What he must be thinking.

She nudged away and dabbed at her eyes. "I'm sorry you had to see me like this. I'll be fine, really."

"On the contrary, I'm glad you didn't come home to an empty house."

She managed the briefest of smiles. "It's just the shock. I hadn't seen it coming."

"If you want my opinion, the guy's about as stupid as they come." He cupped her cheek in his hand and met her eyes. "And his loss is my gain."

His look brought her back to the night before, the sizzling kiss on his patio, the way his hands and lips had worked together to throw her into a lustful, senseless frenzy, and those parting words he'd left her with when she'd fled shortly after.

He hadn't lost that steamy intent, and it revived her initial question.

"What are you doing here?"

He slipped his free hand around her waist and smiled. "I was going to try my hand at getting you to dump that boyfriend of yours. To convince you that we've got something going here, you and me. That if I know anything about people and situations, I'm the guy you need to be spending your evenings with." He shrugged and barely covered a smirk. "But I guess this ex of yours beat me to it."

He tipped her chin up and studied her lips. "Because I'll tell you one thing, Ms. Roth. If you'd shown up at *my* house in this sexy raincoat, the only cries coming from this luscious mouth would have been cries of pleasure."

The lump came back to her throat along with the tears in her eyes. Not over heartbreak, but over the desperate need to hear those words. She'd taken a hit on so many levels, the worst of which had been Rob's comments about their sex life. Only now did she recognize how badly she wanted to hear it wasn't true. That she really could turn a man on and not leave him feeling as though he'd just made love to a comfy old shoe.

Clint leaned in and whispered close to her ear. "What's under the raincoat, babe?"

She swallowed and tightened the belt at her waist. She couldn't take rejection from two men in one night, and trust wasn't something she had in abundance just then.

"I don't th—" The soft press of his lips to her neck stopped the protest mid-word.

"Margot, I haven't been able to stop thinking about you

since you left my house last night." He touched light kisses along the edge of her earlobe, sending a twirling flurry of sparks around her belly. "Just the thought of kissing you again has been driving me to distraction all day. I haven't been able to do anything but want you."

Caressing a finger down her throat, he trailed it over her lapel then gently tugged at the neckline. "Show me what that idiot didn't appreciate and I'll show you what a real man does with a beautiful woman."

There was that word again. Beautiful. Clint thought she was beautiful. And she was so thirsty to hear more, she found herself untwisting the belt and letting the folds of her jacket fall free.

He dropped his eyes to her chest and groaned. And despite his obvious appreciation, the remnants of that horrifying moment at Rob's door still left her trembling with nerves.

"I don't think this—" she started, trying to close the coat back up, but Clint shook his head and tugged it off her shoulders instead. It landed at her heels, and a shiver ran from the back of her neck down to her toes, her body reacting to the chill in the room and the vulnerable state she found herself in. She couldn't take any more hurt tonight, and this move felt too risky to chance.

Slowly, he slipped his hands over her breasts and down her waist, his gaze savoring every inch of her as she stood there flushed and nearly naked.

"Do you have any idea how sexy you are?" he whispered.

"No," she admitted.

He squeezed, and though the pressure was light, it seemed to steal the wind from her lungs.

"I've never wanted a woman as badly as I want you right now." Then he lifted his gaze, allowing his eyes to provide the assurance she couldn't grasp from his words alone. "You turn me on in so many ways, I can't even count them all."

And as if he saw the doubt in her eyes, he moved her hand to his jeans and placed it over a very telling erection.

"Oh!"

He closed his mouth over her neck and suddenly all thoughts of her disastrous evening slipped from her mind, replaced by the memory of last night, and a rush of heat gathered between her legs and spread outward. With his palms circling her bare ass, he moaned and pulled her waist to his.

"Oh, Margot," he begged. "Tell me you want me, too."

Those masterful hands went to work on her body, just like they had the night before. Except tonight, her response wasn't simply desire. Tonight, desire mixed with a thirst to restore her sense of sexuality. To prove Rob wrong and repair the damage he'd done to her confidence. Couple that with the raw chemistry that seemed ever present between her and Clint, and the result was a cocktail of lust and carnal need. Last night, her body wanted him. Tonight, her spirit needed him. And she replied by palming his length through his jeans and giving it a squeeze.

"I want it, too," she confessed.

She'd barely gotten the words out when Clint swung her into his arms and eyed the room. "Where the hell's your bedroom?"

She pointed to an archway and he quickly sped down the hall and into her bedroom where he deposited her on the mattress among a pile of cushy pillows. He surveyed the room, moving over to pull the blinds closed and casting the room in dark shades of gold and umber. Then kneeling down between her legs, he studied her with eyes filled with greed.

"This was fate, you know," he said, brushing his palms up her stomach, over the silky satin of her bustier. "Me showing up like I did, you dressed like this." He bent down and kissed the upper curve of her breast. "You could turn me on dressed in long johns, but this…" He slipped his hands under her and thrust her against his waist. "This is divine intervention."

And just as he had the night before, he went to work on her body and senses, igniting fires everywhere his hands came in contact with her skin. She basked in the raw appreciation in his eyes, the way he treasured her with his hands and assured her with his smile. In his arms, she was a ripe, passionate woman, worthy of admiration and adept at stirring desire. And if there were ever a time when she needed this most, now was it.

This *was* divine intervention. And in acceptance of the moment, she let go of her inhibitions and allowed him to replenish her soul.

As he kissed and nibbled on her flesh, she worked to take his shirt off, needing to see with her eyes the strength that had enveloped her. And when she peeled it off, she couldn't help but gasp.

The man was picture-perfect. Chiseled abs and rock-hard biceps, dusted by a hint of soft hair that started at the center of his chest and trailed down below his belt. She lifted from the bed and pressed her mouth to the solid flesh, loving the salty taste of his skin and the feel of the muscled masses as they moved and contorted against her tongue.

Her heart sped and her sex throbbed, his lustful moans building heat to the point of combustion. She caressed her hands over him, taking in the smooth feel of his skin, wanting to touch and taste and lick and suck every sweet morsel. The simple touch wasn't enough. Nothing seemed like enough as she soaked him in, trying to absorb as much sensation through as many senses as she could.

His fingers came around the left strap of her thong and in one quick yank he snapped it off, as though it were nothing more than a tissue. He tossed it over his shoulder and worked his way down.

"You drive me wild," he said, before digging his teeth into the sensitive flesh of her inner thigh. "I could have this for breakfast every day." Then he slipped out his tongue and ran it straight between her legs.

She let out a cry, the slippery stroke sending quakes up her spine and arching her back.

"Is that too much?" he asked, kissing circles around the spot.

"No. It's—" Her words trailed off in a groan as he took her clit between his lips and suckled. Her toes curled, her eyes rolled back, and she sunk against the soft pillows and let him have his way. His strokes were like velvet, pumping life through her veins and building pressure to a point she anticipated with both excitement and fear. The sparks between them had always been sharp. Now, with his mouth working her most sensitive spots, their naked skin providing no buffers between them, she could only imagine the severity of the climax that awaited her.

He slipped a finger where she wanted his cock to be, and her body arched in acceptance, moving below the level of conscious thought, in a subliminal place where animal instinct ruled. A second finger joined the first, the two sliding in and out through the slippery core while he flicked his tongue over her clit then sucked it into his mouth.

"You're going to make me come," she warned, and he chuckled.

"That's the whole idea."

Each time he slid his fingers inside, her hips thrust to greet them, and Clint began rocking in rhythm with her, encouraging her to keep going, keep moving, keep spinning closer and closer to the edge.

Ripples of pleasure washed over her like waves, ebbing and flowing, each one coming back with more force than the last. She clasped her hands to the bedding and held on, her mind trying to grasp for control but her body getting the best of her. In another time, with another man, she might have fought harder against it. But with Clint, something inside told her to simply follow his lead and let go.

And let go she did.

He pumped faster, pushing her closer to the sweet end, and she huffed out a breathy, "Yessss," encouraging him to keep going, to keep pushing her further.

"Oh," he groaned, "Oh, yeah, babe." And when his moans revealed that he knew she was near, the final climax came swift and hard.

Sucking in a sharp breath, she pulled a pillow over her face and let out a muffled scream. The orgasm took hold fast, shuddering through her, easing, then shuddering through her again in beat after beat of hot ripe pleasure. Until finally, her arms fell at her sides, the only sound in the room her own heartbeat hammering in her ears.

Clint peeled the pillow off her face and tossed it to the ground, then hovered over her, his eyes searching hers for some sign of acceptance.

"Feeling better?" he asked.

She nodded and smiled.

"Can I get you anything?"

"Yeah," she said, the resonant waves still pulsing through her. "I'd like your cock now."

9

CLINT HAD ALWAYS SUSPECTED that when he found the right woman, he'd know it. He wasn't sure why. Maybe because that was the way it had happened for his father, and he and his dad had always been so alike. That Jerry Hilton had even met Jillian Chamberlain was a feat that had beaten the odds. The two had come from such different worlds it was a miracle their paths had ever crossed. But they had one night at a UCLA Bruins game. Jerry had always said that was the night he knew he'd found his future wife. And as Clint looked over the stunning beauty spread out before him, it seemed as though that same fate might have come to him.

Margot Roth was a woman he could spend the rest of his life with. He couldn't explain how he knew. Only that he could feel it in his bones.

With haste, he pulled the condoms from his back pocket, threw off his jeans and slid back on the bed. Gone was the wounded look that had dampened Margot's big brown eyes, replaced by the casual smile of a spirit replenished. And what she didn't know was that he'd barely gotten started.

While her easy visage might be enough for some men, Clint didn't plan to end the night until all her strength was spent, every muscle had turned to mush, and every smidgen of desire was thoroughly answered and spoken for.

He coaxed her into his arms, dotting hot kisses down her

throat as he went to work unfastening the slinky bustier, tiny button by tiny button. It had been a hot turn-on, but for this second round he wanted them both fully exposed.

She touched him all over, running her palms over his chest and snaking her fingers down his arms while purring with a sound that pumped fire through his veins. To be admired by someone that mattered, someone he so wanted to please, added a dose of intensity to every move he made. It put a silly smile on his face and an extra strain on an already throbbing erection.

"I like this," he said, tugging off the last two buttons of the satin lingerie. "But I like these better."

The strapless top fell away, and he cupped a palm around her breast. "These are absolutely perfect."

He took the firm mound in his mouth and tasted the sweetness of her skin. She smelled like fresh soap and flowers, felt like spun silk, and he took his time running his hands over her body, getting acquainted with the many ways he could make her shudder and moan.

He loved how responsive she was to his simple touches. He doubted she knew how sensual she was. She trembled when he pressed his lips to her wrists and gasped when he licked her inner thigh. And when he sucked and nibbled on her breasts, he felt the strength seep right out of her. It was as though he had a magic touch, and with every sigh and shiver, he got harder and hotter for her.

"I want you in me," she urged, sliding a hand between them and grasping his hard cock.

He pulled it back and kissed her fingers. "Babe, we're barely getting started."

"And we're going to finish more than me this time."

He was about to tell her that was all in the plan when she reversed their positions, pushing him onto his back and straddling his thighs.

His stiff shaft stood erect between them and she arched a brow and smiled. The pillows had mussed her hair. One wayward lock hung lazily over her eye and it gave her a sultry bedroom look that shot an extra burst through his loin.

"I can run with this," he conceded.

He slid his fingers up her thighs, but before he reached the apex, she bent in and stroked her tongue up his cock. It was a long, dragging sweep, her eyes never leaving his as she grinned and watched the pleasure wash over his face.

He let out a breath and clenched his fists. Every nerve in his body zeroed in on the silky tongue and that steamy gaze that spoke of carnal intent. It was a look he hadn't seen before and a far cry from the hurt and broken woman he'd found less than an hour ago.

He liked this version, liked the fact that he'd been able to transform her so easily, and he wondered how many more layers of Margot Roth were under that proper surface.

She went down for another pass, electricity pulsing through him as he watched her slow methodical moves. She licked his cock like it was a cool sensuous treat on a hot summer day, and he realized if she wasn't careful, she'd get more than she expected very, very soon.

"Margot," he said, his voice hoarse with warning. "If you want to go for a ride, you need to stop that."

He tossed her a condom and she wasted no time ripping it open and placing it over his tip.

"At your service," she said. Then she took him in her mouth and unrolled the sheath with her lips.

White heat boiled through him as she took him in fully, sliding her tongue all the way to the base and then sucking a path back the way she came.

"Mmm," she hummed, the vibration in the touch nearly breaking him in half.

"Come here." He scooted back until he was upright and leaning against her headboard. "Climb on top of me where I can get my hands on you."

She accepted the invitation, bracing her hands on his shoulders and guiding herself up against the base of his shaft. She was wet, hot and ready, and he grabbed her hips and slid his cock between her folds. She rocked against him in a slow, easy rhythm while he palmed his hands over her ass, circling the smooth mounds before moving on to her thighs and breasts. He loved the feel of her, soft in all the right places, firm and strong everywhere else. This was a real woman, with real curves, a sharp mind and a genuine soul. The kind of woman who could make half a man whole, and as that thought crossed his mind, he clasped his hands to the nape of her neck and pulled her mouth to his.

A soft moan of pleasure came like music to his ears. Was it his or hers, he wasn't sure. But it brought a swell to his chest that told him this was right. This woman, these lips, this sexy body and fiery passion, it was a package that struck the right chords. And when the surety of it washed through him, his heart seemed to unfold.

He opened his mouth and took her in, needing her closer, and as if she understood, she lifted her hips and slid his cock inside.

"Mmm," he groaned, as the slick heat smoothed around him. She sunk down slowly, taking her time until their bodies had fully joined, his sex cloaked in hers and her lulling smile of pleasure heating his blood. It whipped the air from his lungs, the perfection of it, and he held her there steady, needing to simply relish the supple warmth.

"I like the way you fill me," she whispered. "It feels…"

She didn't finish the sentence, kissed his lips instead, but he had the words already. It felt right. The way their bodies came together, the way their mouths formed in a kiss, his palms to her breasts, her thighs to his waist. They fit together like two sides of a puzzle.

Slowly, he moved her hips and they began a steady stroke, churning with a smooth rhythm that broadened and rose. Her eyes grew heavy, her breath labored. And as the tension built, he watched her, wanting to study every expression and soak in every sound. Like a jeweler who comes across a rare and exquisite gem, Clint wanted to examine every facet of this sensual and intriguing woman.

He found a mole at her breastbone and kissed it, trailed his fingers over a dusting of freckles that dotted her shoulders. He made it his mission to find out everything he could about her, starting with what she looked like when she came apart in his arms.

Slipping his hands between them, he circled his thumbs around her clit and a sharp hiss escaped her lips.

"Is that good?" he asked, not really needing an answer. He already had it in the flush spreading across her cheeks. And that was a good thing. With that tousled hair hanging leisurely in her face, her breasts caressing his chest and those delicate fingers digging into his shoulders, she was working him to the point of no return.

"Oh, yeah," she said, and he circled closer, increasing the pressure and letting her own moves stroke the flesh at his thumbs. "Oh…oh, yeah," she repeated.

Her breath turned to pants, and as she upped the speed, streaks of silky pleasure ripped through him. His cock was hard, cresting on the brink of climax, and he went back to studying her, trying to hold on longer.

Her taut nipples rubbed against his chest as she pumped and pumped, rising up and sinking down, up and down, until he had to bite his tongue to stay focused.

"Come, baby," he urged, pushing his thumbs together so that they stroked her most sensitive spot.

"Oh, my—" she cried. "Oh—" It took two more strokes before her clit pulsed and swelled, and he knew this was it.

"That's it, hon," he said. "Let go."

And when she dipped her head and moaned, he cupped her face in his hands and held her.

Those beautiful eyes squeezed shut in tragic splendor, the climax fisting around his shaft, stroking and grinding until he lost himself with her. He tried to hold on, to watch the layers of sensation color her face, but he came too hard, his body jerking and convulsing until all he could do was surrender to the crush.

It tore through him, wave after wave, in a flood of rippling ecstasy. He coiled his hands around her waist and pulled her close, grabbing hold and emptying all he had inside her. The joy and relish in her cries fed the frenzy until the final surge passed and the thrusts began to subside.

She draped her body over his chest, her heavy breath wafting moist heat against his neck, and he slid his hands up her back and dug his fingers into the soft strands of her hair.

Something tightened his throat. Something raw and needy, but also exciting and fresh, and he turned his face to hers and kissed her cheek, drinking in a long breath and soaking in the scent that was uniquely Margot.

And he knew right then that this night was not just fated. This was the night that would change his life forever.

SOMETHING CRUEL and punishing rapped at the edges of blissful sleep, and Margot pulled a pillow over her head to shut it out. She wanted to go back to the lush dreams that had warmed her, the ones involving hot lips and practiced hands. It was a place where smooth music played in a room lit with sensuous candles. Where the rugged scent of sex filled the air and set the mood.

That was a pleasant place, a dream every woman should spend her nights with, and she tugged the blankets up to her chin and tried to go back there.

Then the vile noise returned, coupled with a tapping thing that jostled her shoulder and tickled her waist.

"*Maaarrgot,*" she heard.

The voice was faint, as if it were echoing from the far end of a long tunnel. And it continued to roll on, coming nearer and drawing louder as her heavenly state slipped away.

And then the torrid, venomous creature revealed itself.

Light. Strong, stabbing, hurtful sunlight.

It seeped through her eyelids and pummeled her dreams, and she grabbed for the pillow to shut it out again, but now the pillow was gone.

Squeezing her eyes shut, she reached out for a replacement, but just when she found another it slipped from her hand.

"Oh, no," the voice said. "You need to wake up."

She grunted and turned her face to the mattress. She wasn't a morning person. She didn't like to be badgered out of sleep, and she most definitely didn't like to wake up to the searing, eye-stinging sunshine that was California daylight. Someone had opened the blinds. Someone cruel and inhuman. And she suspected it was the same someone who kept trying to rustle her awake.

"Margot, you didn't set your alarm. It's late. Do you need to be somewhere?"

It was Clint. The man responsible for the divine evening and her slumber of glorious, orgasmic dreams. He'd woken her up several times throughout the night, but all the other times he'd done so by pressing sweet lips to her neck or circling a hot tongue around her nipples, his cock stiff and ready to fill her with pleasure.

She'd welcomed him then, pleased to put the sensual dreams on hold in order to carry them out in the flesh.

And it had been dark.

So where were the steamy kisses? And why, oh, why, was her room filled with that damnable light?

"Close the shades," she groaned against the bedding.

"Margot, it's seven o'clock."

"In the *morning?*"

"Of course. It's late." She felt his hand on her shoulder, warm and inviting. And she wanted that hand back over her body again, but this time it just tugged her awake. "I made coffee. Do you have to get to work?"

She reached for a pillow to throw over her head, but somehow the mattress had been cleared, and she began to accept the fact that her angelic state of slumber was coming to an abrupt end.

Throwing an arm over her eyes, she turned to face the voice. "I don't work before noon."

At least, not unless she had to. It was one of the benefits of being self-employed. She could stop fighting the fact that she was not—repeat, *not*—a morning person and live life the way her internal clock intended.

And according to her internal clock, 7:00 a.m. equated to the middle of the night.

"Oh. I didn't know that."

She felt the bed tip as he sat down beside her.

"Please," she begged. "Close the blinds!"

"Yes, *ma'am.*"

Finally, the torturous light that struck like needles in her eyes dimmed and her mood improved.

"Better?" he asked.

"No. Now I need you back in bed." And when she squeezed an eye open and saw that he'd dressed, she added, "Naked."

He chuckled in that low, sexy tone that brought back a number of memories of the night before. All of them sweet.

"Sorry, hon. I'm late as it is."

"Seven is *late?*"

"In the construction business, half the day's gone by seven."

"That's right," she recalled. "You people and your jackhammers at ungodly hours of the day. I've mentally shot you all a number of times at various stages of my life."

"I don't doubt it. You're not a morning person, are you?"

"No."

"I'll make note of that for next time."

It was only then when he'd mentioned the future that the faint reality of her situation began to creep through the lust and sleep. That somehow during the night she'd lost touch with the gravity of what had happened to her.

She and Rob were through. All the expectations she'd built up over the last month had shattered to pieces. And in the aftermath, she'd ended up in bed with her client, breaking every rule she'd made for herself and her career.

"I need to go," he said. Then he pressed his lips to her forehead and smiled with an expression that was filled with all kinds of assumptions and expectations. "Have dinner with me tonight."

"I don't know…"

"We need to strategize about my mother. We need to get her dating again. The sooner the better. Especially since I can think of a number of things I'd like to do with you in the privacy of my own home."

His eyebrow flicked and he flashed that smile again, the

one that was leaving her unsettled and slightly fearful. There was something in it, a presumption she wasn't ready to deal with and wasn't awake enough to sort through.

"I need to check my schedule."

"Do it and call me this afternoon." Then he pressed his mouth to hers. He'd brushed his teeth and she hadn't, which only added another layer to her discomfort, but he didn't seem to care. Instead, he coaxed her lips apart and probed just like he'd done so many times the night before.

And damned if her body didn't heat up all over again. Apparently, it hadn't caught up with the grim reality her mind was only beginning to wrap itself around.

He tasted of coffee and peppermint and smelled of her bath soap. Apparently, he'd showered as well, and it added to the confusion that was beginning to twist through her.

"I want to see you tonight," he whispered to her lips. "Lunch would have been my preference, but I'm late for work as it is. So I'll have to wait for dinner."

"I might have an appointment already."

"Then come over after."

"I…"

He pecked her cheek and stood, tossing the pillows back on the bed and tucking the blankets up to her chin. "Go back to sleep and call me when you get to work."

She started to think of an objection, then noticed he'd already walked out of the room.

Eyes wide-open and all remnants of sleep dispatched, Margot sank back into the pillows and stared at the ceiling. It was too early in the morning to thoroughly collate what she'd done, but the feeling in her gut said she'd just thrown a mountain of problems onto her already muddled situation.

She wouldn't deny that she'd needed Clint last night. She'd come home so wounded and humiliated, only a man like him could have shoved off her insecurity and unraveled the damage Rob's hurtful words had done. And for that, she owed him thanks.

But the look in his eyes disturbed her. It was a look that said he expected much more. How much, she didn't know. But that uneasy feeling suggested it was probably more than she could deal with at the moment. Possibly ever. It was exactly the reason she always preached to her friends and clients that rebound sex was usually a very bad idea. And now she was faced with the repercussions. Except in her case, the repercussions came with the added complication of a contract and an exorbitant fee she'd already deposited into her savings account.

As the weight of it pressed against her, she clasped the blankets and pulled them up over her head, needing to shut the world out for a few more hours. Seven o'clock was too early for anything, most definitely for all the dire thoughts waltzing into her mind. It was time to go back to sleep, to get more of the rest she needed.

And later, when she was really ready to start her day, she could come to grips with what the hell she'd just done.

10

"MY MOM thinks I keep jumping from man to man because I'm too picky. Do you think that could be true?"

Margot stared at her new client, Wanda, trying to come up with an answer to her question while fighting the overwhelming urge to throw her hands in the air and admit that she didn't have a clue.

She had to believe this type of thing happened to others in her profession—marriage counselors in the midst of divorce, child psychologists with kids they couldn't control, financial consultants on the verge of bankruptcy. Surely other people in her line of work had had days when they wanted to stand up and pronounce, "Sorry, Person Seeking My Help, but I'm just as fricking confused as the rest of you. In fact, if you come up with answers, make me first on the list of people you call."

If counselors had days like that, then today was Margot's day. Because after the night she'd had she didn't feel the least bit qualified to answer Wanda's question.

"Well," she tried, "it's not uncommon for some people to be unrealistic about the success of their relationships."

I, of course, would be one of them.

She gritted her teeth and continued. "Others aren't prepared for the work involved in making a good relationship great."

Now that—that—would be Rob.

"And then," she added, clenching her hands into fists. "Some are simply addicted to the chase and they perpetually play the field in an effort to keep themselves available."

Ladies and gentlemen, please welcome Clint Hilton.

She closed her eyes and sighed. Exactly how much more dysfunctional could her love life get? In one night, she'd somehow managed to corner the market on every love blunder known to humankind.

If she was only dealing with the breakup with Rob, she'd be sitting here wounded and wondering, but still capable of getting through the day. And if she'd simply fallen in bed with Clint as a knee-jerk reaction to being dumped, she could still maintain some rationality over what had happened between them.

But no, it couldn't end with that. She had to throw herself over the edge by admitting that last night was the most spectacular night of sex she'd ever had. That instead of a reaction to the breakup, sleeping with Clint had really been a culmination of sexual tension that had been building since they'd met. That though she'd felt so right about Rob—a man who fit her core principles with textbook precision—she felt even more right with Clint, a rich playboy she was barely acquainted with and with whom she had nothing in common.

And that even now, with the fog clearing and daylight shining a new perspective on life, she was still staring at the phone, aching to call Clint to find out when they could meet for an encore.

That—*that*—was the proverbial threshold she'd crossed to take her from hurt and confused to totally up in arms.

Last week, she'd had her life wrapped up in a clean and tidy package. Today, she was certain of nothing. And as she sat there staring at the befuddled look in Wanda's eyes, she felt completely ill-equipped to offer any advice whatsoever.

"So," Wanda asked. "Which one of those people do you think I am?"

Pulling a heavy breath, Margot sucked it up and went through the motions. "Let's start by getting to know you." She grabbed the in-depth survey from her client package and slid it across the desk. "This questionnaire is designed to get you thinking about what's important to you in a relationship, what you value, how you envision your future. It not only helps me get to know your likes and dislikes, but points out the things you should be paying attention to when you're on a date."

Note that not one of them is how hot the sex is, or how dreamy the guy's big blue eyes are, or how badly you want to get into his pants.

"There is no such thing as a perfect relationship," she went on, sliding a second booklet to her client. "But if you focus on these four core principles—friendship, respect, honest communication and common ground—you'll have the basis on which you can build."

Or not. There's also the jerk factor that could ruin everything. Unfortunately, I haven't developed a brochure for that yet.

She shoved down her cynicism and pushed herself to continue. "Let's start here, and while you're answering the questions think about the relationships in your past. Don't focus so much on the particulars that caused you to think the man you were dating was wrong for you. Focus on the core principles, asking yourself if any or all of them had been in place. Look at your likes and values, and see where they matched and didn't match. Those will be the discussion points for our next meeting, and we can go from there."

She held it together while she and Wanda finished their conversation and scheduled a follow-up meeting for later in the week. And when Wanda left and Margot was alone, she slid into her chair and placed her head in her hands.

Oh, this mental state of hers wasn't going to work at all. Rob had left her bitter and unsure, and before she could clear her mind and get over that issue, Clint had waltzed in and spun her in a whole new direction. The two men had come together and succeeded in destroying her entire belief system, not to mention her professional confidence. And if she didn't get a grip right now, it would destroy her career, as well.

She got up from her desk and stepped through her office, brushing a hand over her client files. Those files represented all kinds of men and women looking for that perfect someone.

And among them were dozens and dozens of success stories, weren't there?

Her rational mind tried to tell her she wouldn't have made it this far if she hadn't known what she was doing. If she had been a hack, Alan would have seen through her and severed their partnership long ago.

What she was going through was just a temporary setback, easily cured if she could step back, take a breath and remove herself from the dating world for a while. She needed to regroup and cleanse, meditate some surety into her soul, put the focus on herself and rethink her priorities. Instead of waiting for Clint's call, she should be calling him up herself, telling him that while last night had been wonderful, it would need to stay a one-time thing.

That would be the strong and right thing to do. The smart thing. The classic Margot move. So without giving it more thought, she picked up the phone and dialed his cell.

He answered on the second ring. "Clint Hilton."

"Hi, it's Margot."

His voice turned playful. "I've been thinking about you all morning. I'm glad you called."

"Yeah, um…I've been thinking about you, too."

"Have dinner with me tonight."

She lowered to her chair. "Oh, Clint, I don't think that's a good idea."

"We need to strategize about my mother. Now that you've met her, we'll need to discuss next steps, tell me what you think."

"Yes…we do need to do that. But, look, I need to talk to you about last night."

He chuckled low and silky. "Don't thank me, sweetheart. The pleasure was most definitely mine. And I can't wait for the repeat performance."

"That's not exactly—"

"I've got a great restaurant in mind. Do you like fish?"

"Well…yes, I like fish, but—"

"Excellent. What time do you want me to pick you up?"

"I—" This wasn't going her way at all. She needed to be clear and up front about where the relationship was *not* going, but just the sound of his voice had her forgetting her own argument. And she knew for a fact that it would not work to try this discussion in person. Not with that tempting mouth grinning at her and those sparkling blue eyes calling her beautiful and those masterful hands mere inches from her—

"Margot?"

She squeezed her eyes shut. "Make it six."

There was no mistaking the sweet victory in his tone. "I'm looking forward to it. The place is casual. My only request is that you wear something that's easy to get out of."

And when she snapped the phone shut, she knew without a doubt she wasn't getting away from Clint Hilton anytime soon.

THE LATE-MORNING SUN was high over Pasadena's Rose Bowl as Clint stepped out of his truck into a parking lot filled to the brim with people attending the Sunday flea market. Despite the fact that Margot had been trying to push back from him all week, he'd managed to insinuate himself into her evenings either by hooking her up with his mother or by coaxing her into a date. It was shameless, sure, but Clint couldn't help it. Each night, he'd learned more and more about her, and each night he grew more and more endeared by what he found.

Yesterday, he'd talked her into a drive up the coast for wine tasting and lunch. They'd put the top down on his antique bathtub Porsche, and he'd treated her to a day of food, drink and shopping à la Clint Hilton.

Today, the tables were turned. They'd traded in his sports car for one of the company work trucks and headed to the Rose Bowl flea market, an event he'd driven past a hundred times, but never experienced up close and personal.

"This place is packed," he said, looking over the sea of cars that surrounded the stadium.

Margot shut the passenger side door and placed a wide-brimmed straw hat on her head. It had a pink and green silk scarf around the band that fluffed into a big puffy bow in the back. It should have made her look cute in a grandma/gardener kind of way, but coupled with the torn jeans cutoffs and crocheted green halter, it only looked sexy as hell.

She placed a pair of wide sunglasses over her eyes. "You should see it before nine. The line starts before sunup to get into this place. People think you can get the best deals by getting here early. I prefer going late, when the vendors are getting antsy about not making their table fees or having to drag all their stuff back home."

He slipped an arm over her bare shoulder. "I think it's that you're a night owl and even the best flea market deals won't get you up and out before noon."

She laughed. "Okay, so maybe you have me there."

The two made their way through the parking lot toward

the front entrance where they paid their admission and passed through the gates. And when they did, Clint had to stand in awe of the sheer enormity of the place. Canvas tents spread as far as the eye could see. Under them, vendors had set up shop selling everything from antique sinks to used CDs to sporting goods and old clothing. He'd never seen anything like it. Practically everything a person could want all in one spot.

Margot stopped and placed her hands on her hips. "Let's start that way," she said, pointing to the right.

"What are we looking for again?"

She rubbed her chin and pondered. "I'm thinking a trunk. Like a chest of some sort. It needs to have plenty of storage and a good surface for decoupage."

"And it's for…"

"The woman at Good Shepherd I'd told you about."

"That's right. Daphne, the single mom."

It was over dinner Thursday that he'd discovered Margot volunteered at a women's shelter. Twice a month, she held group sessions and offered private counseling for women trying to rebuild their lives after recovering from abusive relationships. Daphne was a single mother of two who had just landed steady employment and was moving to a place of her own.

"Yeah. She could use a keepsake chest. Not too big, but sturdy. I've been collecting pictures that represent strength, photos of inspirational women, quotes, special things she'd mentioned over the months that were particularly important to her. My plan was to decoupage a collage under the lid of the trunk as a reminder of what she's capable of achieving."

"That's a nice idea."

"I hope so. I did something similar for another woman a

couple years ago, and the shelter director said she still mentions it every time they talk."

He scanned the giant market. "I'll be shocked if we can't find what you're looking for here."

They strolled past the aisles, stopping on occasion to browse at an item that caught one or the other's attention. It was hard to stay focused, there was so much there, and the place had an energy like he'd never experienced before. All around him, people were bartering over prices, passing cash back and forth and scrupulously surveying the items for sale.

And then there were the smells. Disbursed among the booths were food stands offering everything from churros to sausages and burgers. The scent of grilled meat wafted through the air, and every now and then someone would pass by carrying something that looked delicious.

He rubbed his stomach. "I'm getting hungry."

"We just got here."

"It's almost noon."

She darted to a space that offered a collection of small end tables and began browsing as Clint saddled up next to her.

"Cuanto?" she asked, pointing to one with a marble top and claw-foot legs.

"Cincuenta," the man answered, then shrugged and said, "For you, *cuarenta y cinco."*

She held up three fingers. *"Treinta."*

The man eyed Clint, then shook his head. *"Cuarenta y cinco."*

As she pulled out the drawer and flipped it over, she and the vendor chattered in fluent Spanish, Clint only picking up a handful of the conversation, having forgotten most of what he'd learned in high school years ago.

Finally, she shook her head and waved him off. *"Gracias."*

The man said something else, but she simply took Clint's hand and kept walking.

"If I caught any of that correctly, it sounded like you got him down to forty."

She frowned, though her eyes held a playful smile. "And if you hadn't been with me, I would have got him down to thirty."

He gaped. "What did I do?"

She grabbed his wrist and jiggled his gold Rolex. "You've got 'I can buy this whole market ten times over' written all over you."

"You're telling me I'm dressed too nice?"

"My fault. I should have told you to leave the bling at home."

He laughed, never having his watches referred to as bling before, but not entirely arguing with the sentiment. He supposed in a place where price was negotiable, it was best to look as destitute as possible.

"Should I take it off?"

She looked him up and down. "It wouldn't do any good. You've got the look."

"What look?"

"Like you just stepped out of a Donna Karan ad."

He stopped and held his hands out. "This is just jeans and a shirt."

She coiled her arm in his and prodded him along. "It's not what you wear. Your pores ooze money, and the people who work here can smell it. I'm afraid you're destined never to get the best deal at a flea market."

"That's discrimination."

She laughed. "Welcome to the other side of L.A."

They continued strolling, and while he tried to be bothered by her assessment, he couldn't. Instead, he enjoyed it. He and Margot reminded him of his parents, his father coming from a blue collar working class family and his mother coming from wealth. The two had made a great combination together, always bringing new perspectives to a relationship that might have been one-dimensional without it.

And what he most liked about Margot was that she wasn't intimidated by him or insecure with who she was. That was how his father had been when he'd met the esteemed Jillian Chamberlain, or so Clint was told. Throughout their marriage, Jerry Hilton always knew where he came from and was forever proud of it. And neither his in-laws' money nor the wealth he'd achieved on his own had ever changed that.

Just as he doubted his own money would ever change Margot.

He liked that about her. He liked it a lot.

"You know," he said. "If you want that table, I'll buy it for you."

"If I wanted that table, I would have paid the guy thirty and made you cover the Clint Hilton markup." She looked up at him and grinned. "It's okay. The fact that I've already forgotten about it tells me it wasn't a must-have."

He put his arm back over her shoulder and let her lead him through the market. They spent the next couple hours looking at all kinds of things, stopping to share an occasional bite to eat here and there. They'd found a Bloody Mary bar and couldn't pass up the temptation, using the drinks to wash down a tri-tip sandwich that he'd concluded was the best in town. Or maybe it was just the company and the atmosphere that made the food taste better.

"There's another flea market farther south that has these rolled tacos that are to die for," she said, snagging a slice of meat out from between the bread and tossing it into her mouth.

"You'll have to take me there sometime."

She licked the remnants from her fingers and he watched, getting horny all over again by the purely innocent gesture.

Clint had realized two days ago that when it came to sex with Margot, he was pretty much in deep. Practically everything she did got him hard, and it was a hazard he'd learned to properly dress for. All his nylon shorts were relegated to the back of his closet, at least until he'd had his fill of her. Though he was quickly coming to the conclusion that might be never.

It hadn't taken him long to notice that his affections for Margot didn't stop in the bedroom. He was pretty much a goner when it came to the whole package. He loved who she was, the places she'd been and the work she was doing. She'd met President Reagan. That was cool. And unlike a lot of the women he'd surrounded himself with, Margot did things that mattered. She changed people's lives for the better, made a difference, and didn't let petty things bring her down.

And the more time he spent with her, the more he wanted to stay around her.

He just needed to figure a way to bring her on board. Because it seemed the more he wanted her, the more determined she was to keep their relationship casual.

Taking her chin in his hand, he pulled her to him. "I've got plans for you tonight."

There it was, that little flinch that always clipped her eyes when he suggested doing anything beyond the immediate moment. As if she'd been one foot out the door and he'd just ruined her plan. He hated that blip. He wanted to see excitement instead, and he wondered how much time he'd have to spend with her before that tiny sign of reluctance disappeared.

He opened his mouth and nearly spoke his mind, but his better judgment stopped him. Push too far and he knew Margot was the type of woman who would push right back. So he diverted the urge to speak by taking another bite of his sandwich.

"What kind of plans?" she asked, though her crooked smile said she knew exactly what he had in mind.

It was enough to leave him with an appetite for something besides tri-tip. Tossing the last of it in the trash, he wiped his mouth with a napkin and headed toward the exit. "Let's get out of here and I'll show you."

Their quest for a trunk abandoned, they made their way out of Pasadena and back toward Margot's apartment in Los Angeles.

"A friend opened a new bar last month and I've been promising to go check it out," he said as they merged onto the freeway. "Come with me."

She eyed him with a touch of disappointment. "*That* was the plan you had for me?"

"That was part of it." He glanced at her and smiled. "But first you'll need to change, which will involve taking those clothes off. And you know what happens when you take your clothes off."

"I see you've got this all worked out."

He had. And after a seemingly endless drive, they finally arrived at her apartment and into the quiet confine of her bedroom.

Stripping off his clothes, he tossed his shirt and jeans on her chair as was becoming the habit. Despite Margot's insistence that they keep things casual, her apartment was turning into his home away from home. And unlike other relationships in his past, this time the familiarity wasn't giving him that choking sense of confinement. His relationship with Margot felt welcome and right, and he ached to see that same sense of acceptance in her eyes, too.

Taking her naked body in his arms, he brushed a strand of

hair from her face and kissed her. He wanted to share what was growing in his heart, but he knew better than to speak with words. So he opted for another way, placing her on the bed where he began a slow and sensual seduction. He moved practiced hands and gentle fingers up and down her body, caressing and tasting all the places he'd learned drove her mad. He smoothed light circles on her pulse points, kissed a path under her ear, down her breast, across her stomach and to the sensitive flesh of her inner thigh. He touched and licked until his cock ached and she groaned and writhed beneath him, those dark eyes glazed with pleasure and her body fully surrendered.

She reached between them and cupped him in her palm, smoothing his hard shaft against her silky abdomen in a motion that churned his insides.

"I want this," she whispered. "I need it."

Instead, he answered her request by crushing his mouth to hers. He slid his tongue past her lips, stroking and thrusting as she moaned and rocked. Her breath grew deep and heavy as she lapped and sucked. And when he circled his thumb over her taut, hardened nipple, she broke the kiss and hissed.

"Please," she begged. "Fill me up."

It was the yearning in her voice that had him sheathing his cock and conceding. Spreading her wide, he positioned himself and slid inside, smoothly and deliberately, achingly slow as he touched her face and watched the pleasure roll over her. He loved her this way, that normally serious look abandoned under the weight of need and desire. In this state she was his, and he loved showing her the lengths she could achieve when placed in his care.

She curved her back to greet him, sliding her hands down his hips and guiding him in until their bodies were fully joined. And as he moved into a steady rhythm, he studied her closely and whispered sweet words of affection.

"You're beautiful," he said, pressing light kisses to her lips. "You drive me crazy."

"It's a short trip," she joked, trying to lighten the mood, but he wouldn't go there. This time it wasn't about sex. It was about making that connection that would take what they had from a light fling to something more.

Slipping a hand under her ass, he lifted her toward him and sunk in deeper. "Take all of me," he urged.

She snaked her fingernails against his chest, the sharp touch adding pain to pleasure and heightening his desire. Sensation began to trickle through him, quick bursts of ecstasy rippling from his cock up through his chest.

She squirmed against him, bucking and moaning as her orgasm neared. "Go," he said. "Let it go." And when she cried out and fisted in climax, his own quickly followed.

White heat ran through him. His body arching and thrusting as wave upon wave crashed through him. He'd wanted to watch her, to express without words what was growing in his heart, but he lost his cause in the release. It stripped him of everything, snatching away his control as he spilled and spilled. And only when the waves subsided and his body calmed did he find the will to glance back into those dark chocolate-brown eyes.

Warmed and sated, they greeted him with a smile. And while they didn't quite hold the knowing awareness he'd been going for, he could hardly feel defeated. She wore the expression of a body satisfied and a spirit well fed.

"Wow," she said, trailing a lazy finger along the line of his jaw. "That was amazing."

Her tone was lighter than he'd like, her stubborn will still trying to hold them in a place where she felt safe, but for now, he decided, that was all right. If she needed to move at her own pace, he wasn't going to argue. Not as long as this was his consolation prize.

"Do we really need to go to that bar tonight?" she asked, her voice husky and raw.

"What's my other option?"

Tugging his chin to hers, she slipped him a quick kiss. "More of this."

He rolled to his side and cradled her in his arms, her head coming to rest comfortably on his chest and her body spooned against him. Lying here, still tingling from the climax and the scent of sex in the air, he could really only come up with one answer.

"What bar?"

11

"I HAVE TO TELL YOU, Carmen, this candle party couldn't have come around at a better time." Margot carried two handfuls of empty wineglasses into Carmen's kitchen and deposited them in the sink. "I really needed a girls' night out."

It was going on two weeks now since she and Rob had broken up, and much against her good judgment, she'd spent every one of those nights with Clint. Granted, she wasn't exactly complaining. Capturing the attention of a fun, rich and sexy man had plenty of benefits, and in the last eleven days, she'd been treated to more of them than she'd envisioned for a lifetime.

Which was exactly the problem.

Throughout all the fine restaurants, fancy cars, expensive wine and high-class stores, she couldn't shake the feeling that she was living in a fantasy world that belonged to someone else. Couple that with the relentless attraction she felt for Clint and her head kept telling her that she was heading for another crash-and-burn. Somewhere, a shoe was about to drop, she knew it. She just didn't know where or when. So when she'd looked at the calendar this morning and saw Carmen's candle party, she welcomed the break. Breathing room was exactly what she needed to get her feet back on the ground and her head turned in the right direction.

Margot grabbed a towel and wiped her hands. "That's it

for the dishes. There's just a bowl of corn chips and half a mocha cheesecake left in the dining room." She smiled. "I decided to leave it out. Seemed a waste to wrap it up and put it away when you know we'll just get it back out in an hour."

"You expect it to last an hour?" Carmen asked. She placed the glasses in the dishwasher and wiped her hands. "Let's go sit down. I'm officially exhausted."

They migrated to the living room where Carmen's cousin, Angela, was looking over the orders from the party.

"Man, you got a ton of free stuff!" the girl said. "I need to have one of these parties."

"You need an apartment of your own, *Angelita*. Auntie Emily isn't going to let you throw a party in her house."

"Maybe outside."

Carmen looked at the younger woman and rolled her eyes. "You save your money for tuition. That college you're going to isn't cheap." She took a seat on the couch next to Angela while Margot grabbed her half-empty glass of wine and joined them.

"Thank you for helping me tonight," Carmen added. "This was more work than I'd expected."

Margot waved her off. "It was good seeing your family again. It's been a while. Besides, I needed the change of pace."

"Don't tell me you've already grown tired of Clint."

Margot gave her friend an incredulous look. "Sure, all the shopping, fancy restaurants and expensive wine are getting tiring. I can't wait to get back to my life as a poor person."

Carmen laughed. "I can't believe you took boss man to the flea market. I'm still trying to picture it."

"Actually, he was pretty sweet. If I didn't know better, I'd think he genuinely enjoyed himself."

And that fact had been gnawing at Margot ever since.

Margot had hoped that somewhere in these last couple weeks, she might have gotten this lust for Clint out of her system. Instead, the more time she spent with him, the more she liked him. Somehow, their fleeting one-night stand had turned into a full-blown affair, and no matter how hard she tried to cool things down, it only got hotter.

She hadn't taken Clint to the flea market in the hope of turning him off. She'd really needed to find a trunk for Daphne. But she had hoped his little stroll inside her world would have helped ground her in the fact that she and Clint existed on two different planes. That while they seemed to have developed a good friendship and mutual respect, when it came to her fourth principle, common ground, they flunked with a capital *F*.

Instead, he only showed her how well he fit in no matter where he was or what they were doing.

No matter how hard she tried to keep him from sliding under her skin, he kept finding a way in. And it made it difficult to remember why they shouldn't be a couple. She'd already gotten carried away in one affair that blew up in her face. Now she was heading down the slippery slope of another one, falling even harder for a man with whom she had even less in common.

"Well, let me go with you two next time. I need to see it with my own eyes."

"I doubt there'll be a next time. You said so yourself, Clint doesn't do permanent. And that's a good thing. As soon as I can be done with this contract of ours, I need to take a break. Did I tell you Rob called the other day?"

Carmen gaped. "No."

"He wanted to meet for coffee so he could apologize in person for how he'd handled things."

"Did you go?" Angela asked.

"No. He's over and done with as far as I'm concerned."

"Oh, you should have gone! You could have ordered a big scalding hot coffee, then poured it right on his junk."

"Angela!" Carmen scolded, though the three women couldn't hold back the giggles.

Margot grabbed a throw pillow and stretched out on the couch. "What I *need* is to be over and done with *all* men for a while. I really hope this date goes well tomorrow night. I need to get Jillian on her way to new relationships so I can move on."

Over dinner the other night, Margot and Clint had managed to talk Jillian into a double date with them and Bo Granger, a man Margot thought would be perfect for her. And to both their surprise, Jillian agreed to go. Now, all she needed was for the date to go well. If the two hit it off like Margot hoped, she'd be one step closer to ending things with Clint.

"Everything tells me I've got the perfect man for Jillian," she added. "But I'm not exactly batting a thousand lately."

"Stop doubting yourself, already. You're good at what you do, Margot. What happened with Rob didn't change that. If you think Mrs. Hilton will like this guy, I'm sure she will." Carmen sipped her wine. "Where are the four of you going?"

"Bo made reservations at the 380 Club."

"Oh, my god, I heard that place is the bomb," Angela gushed. "They have, like, Frank Sinatra impersonators, with real bands, and there's a big dance floor. It's supposed to be totally sick." She eyed Carmen and grinned. "Hey, maybe that's where we'll go for my twenty-first birthday."

Carmen scoffed. "Where is your money tree? That place costs a fortune. Mike and Kelly went there for their anniversary. She said it was over three hundred dollars just for the two of them."

"I'm worth it."

"Start working overtime, honey."

"If you'd fix me up with Brad, I wouldn't need the job *or* college."

"Who's Brad?" Margot asked.

"Our summer intern at H & H," Carmen said. "Angela ran into him at the office last week and has been badgering me ever since to fix them up on a date."

"He's so hot," Angela said, her face brimming with lust.

"He's not for you, *neña*. The boy's a player and he'll break your heart. Besides, he's on the verge of getting fired, anyway. Stan won't let him on the job sites any more after yesterday."

"Clint told me about him, but I didn't hear about yesterday. What happened?" Margot asked.

"Jorge showed him how to use a table saw and put him to work cutting boards. Brad didn't write down the measurement and screwed up over a thousand dollars' worth of lumber before they caught the error." She shook hear head. "Poor kid. He seems sweet enough, but Clint's running out of patience with him and Stan won't let him near a construction site, period. Next week, they're going to try having him work in the office with me."

Angela brightened. "He'll be with *you* all week?"

"Down, girl. Money or no money, you can do better. Besides, we aren't talking about Brad. I want to hear about this fancy dinner you're going to tomorrow night." She pointed a finger at Margot. "What are you wearing?"

Margot shrugged. "I don't know. I haven't thought about it."

"Wear the Jackie O dress."

"You think?"

"It's totally Rat Pack and you look gorgeous in it. You'll have Clint clawing to get you in bed before the night is through."

Margot sighed. "That's not my goal, Carmen. In fact, I

wouldn't mind cooling things down a bit. I can't deal with another relationship on the heels of Rob."

"Don't worry. Clint's not a relationship kind of guy. And you've got the exact right attitude. Have fun with the man for a while. Let him help you get over Rob, get your confidence back, and when this business with his mother is over, you can take your break and focus on *you* for a while."

That was exactly Margot's plan. She'd already deemed it useless trying to keep her distance from Clint while pretending they were dating. He'd somehow managed to hold her under his spell, and no matter how many times she tried to pull away, she couldn't do it. After three days, she'd finally stopped trying and had surrendered to the affair, telling herself to take life one day at a time.

It was a decent idea. After all, she'd done temporary before and had had a fine time with it. As long as she kept herself grounded and didn't get carried away, she'd be able to thank Clint for the time they shared, then walk away when their business was done.

She only hoped that when the day came, it would be as easy as it sounded.

DAYLIGHT WAS just peeking over the hills to the east when Clint slipped on his running shoes and stepped out of his bedroom. This was the first time in almost a week he'd been able to get his run in before work when he preferred. Not that he was complaining. Lately, he'd been getting his morning exercise with Margot, having to postpone his daily jog on the beach until later in the day. He would have been in the same situation today, but Margot had spent the evening with Carmen last night.

He had to admit to having been disappointed when she'd said she had other plans, but in retrospect, he supposed the short break might do them good. It would make tonight all that much better.

He crossed the living room toward the front door, but the unexpected aroma of coffee brewing had him detouring to the kitchen where he found his mother at the bar, thumbing through the newspaper dressed in her pink silk pajamas and matching slippers.

"You're up early," he said.

"Pom Pom woke me up. Somehow, the neighbor's cat managed to climb up to my balcony. It sat there and taunted Pom Pom through the glass until I had to get up and shoo it away."

"I'm sorry. I can talk to Ray if you'd like."

She waved it off and smiled. "I'll talk to him myself if it becomes a habit. In the meantime, why don't you sit down and tell me how you're doing."

He poured himself a cup of coffee and took a seat at the bar. "Good. Life is good. I'm looking forward to our date tonight."

"My son and I on a double date. Who would have figured?"

He squeezed his mother's hand. "None of us expected you to end up alone, that's for sure. But I'm glad you've agreed to go out. It'll be good for you, Mom."

"I suppose." She took a sip of her coffee. "Isn't it ironic that you started dating a matchmaker and only a couple weeks later I'm being fixed up with an eligible bachelor?"

"Margot isn't a matchmaker. She's a dating counselor."

"Semantics. She told us herself at dinner the other night that she often puts singles together. That's a matchmaker."

"Well, call her what you will. I still think it's a good idea that you meet this guy. Who knows? You two might hit it off. And if not, you got out of the house and did something different for a change."

"Oh, I completely agree." She gave him a sideways glance. "What I don't understand is why, if you wanted me to start dating again, you didn't simply suggest it. You didn't need to go through the ordeal of pretending you're dating this woman."

The comment took him by surprise but he managed to smoothly feign ignorance. "I'm not pretending to date Margot. Why would you think that?"

"Clint, you're thirty-one years old. When are you going to accept the fact that I always know what you're doing?"

He took a slow sip of coffee to hide behind his cup. "I have no idea what you're talking about."

His mother slid off the bar stool and poured herself a refill. "I'm not stupid. I've known this relationship of yours was a farce since that first day you brought her home."

"My feelings for Margot are completely sincere."

At least *that* wasn't a lie. Though how his mother figured all this out still had him baffled.

"I'd certainly like to believe that. God knows, she's the first woman you've ever dated that I could actually stomach as a daughter-in-law. And that's exactly why I don't like what you're doing."

"*What* am I doing?"

She put the pot back on the warmer and leaned against the counter. "Using that lovely girl to find me a gentleman friend. And don't tell me you aren't because I'm not that dumb. I knew the moment I saw her you wouldn't have given that girl a second glance had you really met her in a deli. She's not your type—*which is a compliment to her,* mind you." His mother reclaimed her seat at the bar. "Really, Clint, did you think I was born in a barn?"

He pressed his lips together and studied his mom closely, trying to calculate a convincing denial but coming up empty.

"Okay, fine," he conceded. "Yes, I hired Margot to find you a man."

The lack of victory in her eyes said she hadn't been bluffing. She truly had seen through him. And just like the time when he was twelve and had snuck across town to Rickey Stephens's house, he had no idea how she knew.

And just like that time nineteen years ago, she had that same disappointed look on her face.

"Why didn't you just ask me if I'd like to meet with Margot?"

"Ha!" This was where he had her. "After what happened between you and Marge? There's no way you would have agreed to see a matchmaker."

She folded her hands primly. "Maybe not."

"Maybe?"

"But that doesn't change the situation as it stands. Now that the truth is out, you can call off the farce before that poor girl gets hurt."

"What are you talking about?"

"Clint, I like Margot. I like her a lot, and I don't like what you're doing to her. I see the way she looks at you. The woman is falling for you."

He grinned. "You think?"

She frowned. "I *know.* She's head over heels for you. It's written all over her face. Now, I don't know who you're *really* spending your nights with." She placed a hand on her heart. "Please tell me it's not *actually* Margot."

"Yes, it's *actually* Margot, and what's wrong with that?"

"Oh, Clint," she said disgustedly.

"I happen to be very serious about her."

"Don't tease me like that. It's not funny."

"I'm not! I like her. *A lot.*"

She waved him off. "Oh, please. I gave up on that fantasy a long time ago."

"What fantasy?"

"You ending up with a normal woman I'd actually be proud to call my daughter-in-law. I've turned my hopes to Nate for that."

"Huh, you can take the fantasy back because I'm serious about her, more serious than I've ever been with a woman before."

There was a long silence while Jillian stared at him, searching his face for some sign that he was playing her. Except when it came to Margot, there weren't any games to be played. He *was* serious about her. Now, he just needed to figure out how to get her to feel the same way.

"You aren't joking," Jillian stated.

"No, I'm not."

She grinned. "That's wonderful!"

With a new bounce to her step, she got up, and went to the fridge and began putting out fixings for eggs. "I loved her the moment I saw her, you know. I just never dreamed you'd be smart enough to end up with someone like her."

"Gee, thanks. And don't get out the champagne yet. She's not exactly jumping into my arms."

"That's ridiculous. She's crazy for you. I see it in her eyes every time she looks at you."

"Maybe. But she's also so skittish thanks to this ex-boyfriend of hers, I don't dare go making any grand gestures. She'd go fluttering off like a bird." He told her about the breakup Margot had gone through and the half-dozen times she'd insinuated that she needed to take a break from romance as soon as their contract was satisfied. Granted, she'd never been perfectly blunt about it, but he'd read the signs and gotten the picture. And the more he grew to care for her, the more that fact kept needling him in the jaw.

How ironic that for most of his adult life, he'd gone out of his way to keep his relationships casual, and now that he'd finally found a woman he really cared for, she refused to take him seriously. And the worst of it was he had no idea what to do about that. Never did he think he'd find himself in a position of having to sell himself to a member of the opposite sex.

He was Clint Hilton, after all. He wasn't exactly versed in having to prove himself worthy. And while he had managed to keep her in his bed, he knew that elusive heart of hers was still heavily guarded.

"Give her time," Jillian advised. "She's been through a bad experience. It doesn't surprise me that she's cautious about getting involved with someone else so soon. But I'm sure she'll come around as you two continue to get to know each other."

"And that won't happen if you go spilling the beans that you know about this. So if you like Margot as much as you say you do, you need to keep pretending you don't know anything about my contract with her. Go on this date, keep playing along."

"I hardly see why that's necessary. Wouldn't it be better for everyone if—"

"No, I need more time to bring her around. Trust me on this. This little arrangement of ours is working in my favor."

His mother stared him down, her expression saying she didn't like what he was asking at all. But he could also see the wheels turning in that brain. She liked Margot as much as he did, and he doubted very much she wanted to risk being the one to ruin it for them both.

"What choice do you give me?" she finally concluded. "I'll go along with it tonight. For now, that's all I'll promise."

He smiled and kissed her cheek. "Then I'll have to make tonight special, won't I?"

12

THE 380 CLUB was a pricey throwback to the famous Las Vegas lounges of the 1950s. Front and center in the oversized dining room was a stage set up for live music. Below it, the parquet floor offered couples the option of sharing a dance while surrounded by diners enjoying a fabulous steak-house meal. The perimeter of the room was lined in half-circle red vinyl booths, tufted with brass buttons and high along the back for privacy. It looked like a place where Joe DiMaggio might have taken Marilyn Monroe for a date, and Margot couldn't help feeling that any moment Steve Lawrence and Eydie Gorme would go strolling by.

The dress was formal. Men weren't allowed in without a jacket and the women sported heels in a refreshing departure from Los Angeles's ever-casual restaurant scene.

"I've never seen a real Baked Alaska," Margot mused, as a black-vested waiter strode along carrying one on a tray.

"I don't think I have either," Clint said. He surveyed the room. "I keep expecting Dean Martin to show up."

Margot almost choked on her cabernet as she laughed. "I was just thinking the same thing."

"This place is pretty amazing."

"You've never been here?"

He shook his head. "No."

Bo and Jillian had excused themselves to the dance floor, giving Clint and Margot a moment alone.

"So what do you think of Bo?" she asked.

"I like him. He's nothing like my dad, which is a good thing. Mom will do better if she doesn't try to find a replacement for what she had, and a guy like Bo is perfect. He's different, but in a good way."

"I was hoping for that."

He smiled. "You scored."

The warm expression on his face erupted a tiny cyclone in her stomach, pretty much like it did every time she was near him, and she wondered if that would ever go away. He looked strikingly handsome tonight in a tailored gray suit that brought out the tiny silver flecks in his blue eyes. A collarless navy blue dress shirt framed the hard lines of his jaw, steeling his already muscular chest while adding a youthful flair to the classic style. He'd tousled the tips of his sandy blond hair, probably haphazardly when he'd dressed, though each strand looked as if it had been meticulously placed for a photo shoot.

Put together, the package was potently sexy and deliciously sharp. Like a well-paid corporate executive with a chic but rugged edge.

"What's the story of his marriage?" Clint asked. "He didn't say much about it."

"His first wife died of cancer a number of years back. From what I understand, his second marriage was short-lived and didn't work out at all. She'd been more interested in his money than him. I went to school with his daughter and she encouraged him to see me about making better choices."

"Mom definitely won't care about his money."

"No, and he won't care about hers. He isn't on the Chamberlain scale, but he does well for himself as a stockbroker."

"It sounded like it."

Bo and Jillian returned to the table all smiles and slid into the booth.

"Your mother's being kind," Bo said. "I'm certain I stepped on her toes at least twice, but she keeps denying it."

"He did not," Jillian replied. "But he did let me lead."

She had a blush on her face and a sparkle in her eyes, two good signs that the date was going well. And it was, for all Margot could tell.

Bo Granger was a tall, stocky man who ironically looked and sounded like a young Tony Bennett. Or maybe it was the atmosphere that brought the famous singer to Margot's mind. Either way, he had those similar rugged good looks and a perpetually jovial manner that made him fun to be around.

And most importantly, he and Jillian seemed very comfortable with each other. Not once had Clint or Margot had to chime in to fill up an awkward silence or failing conversation. It turned out that Bo and Jillian could have easily handled the date alone, though Margot had to admit that being here personally to witness their good time was doing wonders for her confidence. A success story viewed firsthand to remind her that she was capable and qualified, that she could more often than not put two people together and have it go well.

"How about giving me a shot on the dance floor, Mom?" Clint asked, holding a hand out for his mother.

Jillian smiled. "I'd love that."

The two went off leaving Bo and Margot strategically alone.

"Well?" Margot asked, taking a sip of her wine.

"I like her," Bo said. "I think my daughter was right in singing your praises. I'm really enjoying myself tonight." He held up his glass and clinked it with hers. "I'd love to see her again if she's interested."

"Jillian seems to be having a good time, too."

He laughed. "She might not want to dance with me again. I really am a horrible dancer. All my best moves are reserved for the golf course."

"I think she golfs."

"Really?"

"Yes, I'm almost positive she'd mentioned it."

The two continued to make small talk while the band played "Luck Be a Lady," and when the song was over, Clint coaxed Margot to share the next dance with him.

The tempo slowed to a soft ballad, and Clint placed a hand around the small of her back and pressed her against him. Even in heels, she only came eye level to his chest, and she had to tilt her chin to look up at him. "Is your mom enjoying her date?"

"I think so."

She frowned. "Come on. I know you grilled her while you two were dancing. What did she say?"

His laugh vibrated against her chest. "She's having a great time. You did good, putting them together."

Margot sighed with relief. "Oh, I hope so. Jillian's far too young to spend the rest of her life as a single widow. She's got too much to offer."

"Hey, just getting her out dating is more than I'd expected so soon. You've done well, Margot."

"It would be nice if things work out between Jillian and Bo. She can start the second chapter of her life, and you can be done with me and get back to the life you had before your mom moved in with you."

A perplexed look came over him. "I'm not exactly sure I want that life again."

"Well," she chuckled somewhat awkwardly. "You know what I mean."

Slowing the rhythm between them, he placed a warm hand against her cheek and held her gaze. "I'm not sure I'll ever be done with you."

She stared into his eyes and saw nothing but stone-hard seriousness.

"Really, Margot. I'm enjoying the time I spend with you."

Though it sounded clichéd, she wondered if he said that to all the women he dated. Were such comments simply part of the game? Margot had no idea. Ever since they'd met, she'd felt out of her league, like a quarter-slot player suddenly seated at the high-roller table with a big stack of someone else's chips. She wasn't sure how the game was played, didn't know how much credence to put into those words, despite the fact that everything in his gaze told her he meant business.

Still, she tried to lighten the moment with an easy smile. "I'm enjoying your company, too."

Though she'd spoken the words casually, it hadn't changed the scorching look in his eyes, nor had it lessened the giddy feeling he gave her. He wasn't flinching or backing down, and for what seemed like a long while, they moved to the slow tune and stared into each other's eyes.

"I say we wrap this dinner up so I can get you alone," he whispered when the music ended. "I've had a rough week at work, and my bed was cold and empty last night." Pressing warm lips to hers, he asked quietly, "Come home with me tonight?"

And when she opened her mouth, she found herself spilling the same words she'd been saying for two weeks. "I'd love to."

IT WAS AFTER TEN by the time Clint and Margot had made it back to his house and retreated to his bedroom, and though she'd been there before, the vast expanse of the room still left her in awe.

One wall continued the floor-to-ceiling glass windows that stretched across the back of his house, providing a view of the city and access to the pool and terrace. A large white marble fireplace took up another wall and a king-size bed in the center of the room sat on a low platform, making it appear as though it were floating on air. The dressing area and master bath disappeared around one corner, and at the far end of the room, a small terrace exposed a view to a side yard she hadn't known was there.

"Why don't you get comfortable?" he suggested. "And by that, I mean naked."

His smile was filled with promise, and she kicked off her sandals while he pulled the drapes, cutting off the view to the backyard and enclosing them in privacy. Moving to the side entrance, he opened the large glass doors and turned on a set of low patio lights, then hit the jets to the secluded spa.

Curious to see the small terrace, she stepped over for a closer look. Clint tossed off his suit jacket, then slipped up behind her. "You looked beautiful tonight," he said, tugging the dress off her shoulders and letting it pool at their feet. "Did I remember to mention that?"

She turned, now clad only in a matching set of black lacy underwear that left him groaning with appreciation.

"About a dozen times."

He slid his fingers through her hair and kissed her deeply. "I know I thought it about a hundred times," he whispered to her lips. "I just wasn't sure how often I said it out loud."

She grinned and began tugging at the buttons of his shirt.

"Let's get wet," he said. He backed away and tore off his clothes while Margot slipped out of her lingerie and headed onto the patio. A low wall sheltered the area on two sides while still leaving the canyon exposed. The night air was nearly still, with only the faintest breeze rustling the leaves of the palms and crape myrtles that framed the yard. Down through the canyon, lights from the streets and houses twinkled like stars, and Margot stepped into the spa and took in the spectacular view.

"Oh, this is what I've been waiting for." Clint groaned as

he stepped in behind her and sunk in front of the jets, cupping his hands with water and rushing it over his face. Droplets formed tiny rivers down his neck and over the planes of his chest, and she watched them as they trickled toward the surface.

He had to be the sexiest man she'd ever seen naked, just the sight of him getting her primed for whatever he might have in mind.

She moved next to him, letting her head fall lazily back while the soft rushing water soothed her shoulders and back. If this wasn't a slice of heaven, she didn't know what was.

"You said something about a rough week at work," she said, closing her eyes as one of the jets pummeled the base of her spine.

"The worst." He shifted slightly, then closed his eyes and sighed when the rushing water hit the right spot. "Brad, my intern, is determined to drive me bankrupt."

"Carmen told me about the lumber incident. It sounds like he's having a hard time catching on."

He laughed. "That's putting it nicely."

He told her about the trouble Brad had been causing all week, how he and Stan would have fired the kid if it weren't for his good friend and investor, Edward. She listened as he recounted every incident, offering advice where she could and an understanding ear when there was nothing more to say. And while they chatted, a cozy feeling of familiarity came over her.

These were exactly the moments she'd thought she couldn't share with a man like Clint. And in the aftermath of all her fears and confusion, she began to question why. Sure, the visions of her in a marriage hadn't included reflecting over the day while naked in a spa overlooking West Holly-wood. Nor had she expected the day's events would include multimillion-dollar investment deals, high-risk contracts and investor relations. But peel away the particulars and what was underneath amounted to the same thing. Two people sharing their lives, supporting each other through the ups and downs of living, coming together to build strength they couldn't achieve on their own.

It felt familiar and right, their conversation grounded by all the things that should really matter, like trust, affection, admiration and respect.

"Bottom line is, the kid's a spoiled trust-fund baby," Clint said. "If I can just make it through the summer, he'll be off my plate."

She raised a brow. "It's May. Summer hasn't even started yet."

"I don't have any choice."

"Of course, you do. You can talk to Edward. You aren't doing him any favors by pretending everything's fine with his grandson. It's quite possible that as a friend, he's expecting honesty from you."

"You could be right."

"I know I'm right."

He quirked a half smile. "You're that sure of yourself, huh?"

"My expertise with relationships isn't limited strictly to dating."

He snaked an arm around her waist and pulled her onto his lap. "No, I'm aware of your many talents. I particularly like the way you roll on condoms."

He adjusted his cock between her legs, and by the feel of things, he was nearly ready for one.

"You liked that, huh? I saw a woman do it in a movie once."

That perked his interest.

"Oh, really? What else was in this movie you saw?"

She smiled and slid a wet finger over his lips. "It was quite erotic."

Propping up on her knees, she leveled her breasts with his lips, and he wasted no time in cupping them with his hands and taking a bite. Steam rose off her skin, encircling them in a mist of fog and water and sex. The cool air pricked at her skin, heightening the sensation when Clint took one nipple in his mouth and slicked it over with wet heat.

"The man was very well endowed, much like yourself," she said, lolling her head to the side as he moved from one breast to the other. "The woman really got it on when he put it inside her."

Clint groaned.

"She especially liked to lick it. She did that a lot."

He slid his hands under the water and grasped her waist, pulling her against him and using his teeth to graze her wet skin. Amid the warm swirls of rushing water and Clint's erection pressed against her sex, she ached to lift up and slide him in. But they needed protection.

"How far away are the condoms?" she asked.

He reached behind him and patted around until he came up with a handful of foil pouches.

"I planned ahead."

She noted the number. "I guess I'll have to tell you about the movie's sequel, too."

He chuckled and let them drop back on the terrace, then went back to his feast. "Tell me more," he said, his voice growing husky and low.

She slid her hands over him, enjoying the feel of his chest and arms, silky skin over firm muscle, shifting and contorting under her fingers as they moved and caressed. The temperature of her blood climbed until an occasional wisp of air brushed up the canyon and nipped at the back of her neck, sending a tingle down her spine. Then the breeze settled and the heat rose again, starting the cycle over, hot then cold then hot again. It brewed her into a frenzy of lust and need as Clint worked magic with his hands and lips.

"The woman," she said, her own voice getting breathy, "liked it fast and hard."

His cock twitched against her thigh. "Fast and hard, huh?"

She nodded and sunk her teeth into the tender flesh just under his ear. "And she liked it most when he took her from behind."

"Behind," he repeated.

"She said it was tighter and deeper that way."

Clint's fingers began to tremble as he cupped her face in his hands and whispered, "You're driving me crazy."

He crushed his mouth to hers, stroking his tongue deep and circling fast, wrapping his arms around her and holding her tight until he'd thoroughly stolen her breath.

She reached behind him and came up with a foil packet.

"I think I should *show* you the rest."

Without any more prompting, he nudged her off his lap and stood, rivers of water cascading over his abs and steam billowing off his shoulders as he opened the package and sheathed himself.

She turned and hugged the edge of the spa, wiggling her ass in invitation and glancing over her shoulder.

"It went something like this," she said.

The muscle in his jaw twitched. He grasped her hips. Mist embroiled them both, adding a sinister quality to the dark fire she saw smoldering in his eyes. And when he pulled her sharply against his shaft she gasped, ready for the fullness her body ached for. But instead of sliding inside, he prodded her to move to the left.

"This way," he said, pointing her toward the edge where the privacy wall scaled down to expose the sweeping view of the canyon. She thought he'd nudged her over to take advantage of the sight, but when he guided her waist down, she realized there was more to this spot than the view.

A bubbling rush of water streamed between her legs, pulsing wet heat to her clit and beyond. Clint lowered his cock behind her and groaned in sweet satisfaction.

"Right there," he said.

The two gyrated around the jet, a sharp sensation whipped through her every time the water rushed between her legs. The feeling was marvelous, the setting amazing, and when Clint prodded her entrance and poked the tip of his cock inside, she nearly came apart before they started.

"Oh, yeah," she moaned, arching her back to give him better access.

She felt the press of his mouth to her back, slippery kisses trailing between her shoulder blades. He slowly eased inside her, stretching and filling her until he was fully seated, his hips coming to rest against the back of her ass. She took in a sharp breath as her body adjusted to the depth, and he bent over her, gliding his hands over her chest and dipping his mouth to her ear.

"She liked it hard and fast, you said?"

She could hear the strain in his voice. It matched her own sense of urgency as the whirling stream of water circled around her clit and bubbled over the place where their bodies met.

"Please," she begged.

Her wish was his command. Slowly, he slid his cock out, then pushed it back in, out and in, starting at a gentle, languid pace and then building speed. Low moans accented every beat, and each time he sank in fully, his hips thrust her closer to the massaging jet.

He held her tightly, water spattering between them as he

stroked, and soon, her light panting began to deepen into coarse, needy sobs.

His body slapped against hers, thrusting her sex against the jet then pulling it back again, the motion pushing her to a limit she'd never experienced before. The climax built and built, rising higher and higher until she clamped her hands to the edge of the spa and tried to catch her breath.

"I can't stop it," she warned. But he just kept thrusting. The churning water swirled against her breasts, steam soothed her lungs, and the buoyancy of the tub made her feel light as air. It was like a thousand hands working her, a thousand tongues licking her, and with every push of his cock came a thousand more.

She tipped her toes back and coiled her feet around his calves, holding on to the side as the hot stream rushed against her sex and tumbled her toward the edge. And then the deep wave of climax rushed forward.

"Oh, I'm—"

"Go, baby," he urged. "Go."

And when he thrust her toward the jet one last time, she came apart.

She bit her tongue and tried not to cry out, but the throaty groan couldn't be silenced. The climax gripped her every muscle, clamping hard around him and breaking the rhythm he'd settled into.

"Oh." His hands and legs trembled as they began to give in to the pressure. He grasped her hips tighter to regain control, but it was too late, and his own release came quick and hard.

He cried out, snaking his hands around her waist and holding on while their bodies moved together in uncensored pleasure. Over and over, bursts of white heat filled and ebbed, speeding over her then sweeping back, rushing in and out in smooth layers of blissful release.

She pushed against the edge of the tub and into his arms, and he wrapped his hands around her thighs and spilled into her. His breath brushed moist heat against her neck as he grunted and gasped. And then slowly, the frenzy calmed, breath by heavy breath.

He backed them up and sunk down onto the curved seat they'd been in before. For a long while he held her there, still impaled on his shaft, while he kissed her neck and smoothed light fingers over her stomach.

"That was fantastic," he said.

But for Margot, it was more than fantastic.

It was...*perfect.*

She leaned against him and reflected over the last two weeks, and for the first time, allowed herself to admit what she hadn't wanted to face.

She really liked Clint Hilton. More than she should. No matter how much he wasn't fitting her personal profile, he kept slinking into her heart, catching her when she didn't expect it and filling her life with joy. He was warm and comfortable, funny and kind. A treasure in mind and spirit with a golden touch in bed.

And as they stayed there together, their bodies sedated and joined, an emotion came over her too strong for words. Something that both excited and scared her, deep and pure, that felt a little like love. And she knew right then, she'd done exactly what she hadn't wanted to do.

She'd fallen overboard for Clint Hilton.

13

CLINT WHISTLED as he walked through the doors of H & H Associates Monday morning, greeting Carmen with a wide smile and a dozen cream-cheese pinwheels.

"You stopped at Rosie's," she said, eyeing the box. "What's the occasion?"

He set it on the reception desk and she quickly grabbed a letter opener, cut through the gold foil seal and peeked inside.

"No occasion. Can't I treat my favorite office manager once in a while?"

"You could do it more often," she teased. She got up and went to the break room, emerging a few moments later with napkins and a fresh cup of coffee that she handed to Clint. "I heard things went well Saturday night. Did your mom like this guy Margot fixed her up with?"

"I think so. They were supposed to talk today about maybe seeing each other again. We'll see if the guy actually calls."

"And what did you think of him?"

Clint nodded and took a sip from his mug. "I like him. He's a self-made man like my father, but everything else about him is different—in a good way. I think it would have been hard for her if he'd been too similar to Dad. She needs something new, and I think a guy like Bo is exactly the ticket."

"I told you Margot was good. Didn't I tell you she was the best?"

She had. And Clint had more to thank Carmen for than simply the match for his mom. The woman may have very well found him his own future wife, too.

"You'd only been looking for some tips on how to find a man for your mother," Carmen went on. "And in three short weeks, she didn't just give you some advice, she handed you the man."

"That she did."

Carmen pulled a pastry from the box, leaned over and bit into it, sending puffs of fluffy white powdered sugar over her desk. The cheese pinwheels were a mess, but deliciously worth it, and Clint grabbed two for himself and set them on a napkin.

"That's great," she said. "With your mother now occupied, I'm sure you'll be looking forward to getting your old love life back."

"Actually, I kind of like the way it's going right now."

The expression on her face turned.

"What?" he asked.

She shook her head and tried to look innocent. "Nothing."

"That's crap. You're thinking something. What is it?"

"Just…" She finished swallowing the treat, then wiped her mouth. "Be careful with Margot. She's not one of your usual conquests. She's been hurt and she's not in a frame of mind to think clearly." He opened his mouth, but she held up a hand and added, "Really, I think your coming along when you did was the best thing for her. I really do. But I know she's looking forward to being done with this contract so she can step back and take a break."

"She told you that?"

Carmen must have heard the shock in his voice because she took her time to answer. "She's very confused right now. I know she's planning on not dating for a while when this is all over, which has to be a bonus for you. I mean, come on, boss man. We both know you like your freedom."

"Well, I might just be deciding my freedom is overrated."

She scoffed.

"I'm serious," he defended. "I like Margot. She's more than just a fling for me."

Carmen opened her mouth, then closed it, then opened it again. "Clint, please. She's been through a rough spell. She doesn't need any more heartache."

Now he was getting annoyed. First his mother, now Carmen. Exactly how bad a reputation had he made for himself? "I don't intend to give her more heartache."

"I know you don't intend to, but things happen. Don't throw something at her she's not ready to deal with. She's in a fragile state. Be sure of what you want from her before you go making any moves."

He studied her for a long moment.

"That's all I'm saying," she added.

Irked, but left with no argument, he picked up his pinwheels, stepped into his office and closed the door. He knew Margot had been harboring reservations, but he thought this weekend had changed that. Yet, it sounded from Carmen as if that wasn't the case. It seemed as though everyone was dismissing this relationship of theirs just because he'd chosen to spend most of his adult life playing the field. But he was done with that. In fact, every day he spent with Margot he became more and more certain she was the one he wanted to be with for the rest of his life. He could see it so clearly. But could she?

Carmen was right. He wasn't sure what was going through Margot's head, but he knew he had to play this carefully, which meant he needed more time. Time he wouldn't have if his mother and Bo Granger hit it off.

He tried to brush off his concerns by eating his pastries and making some calls, but over the next hour, Carmen's words wouldn't stop gnawing at him. So Margot intended to take a break from dating for a while. He had a hard time believing it.

But a voice inside told him not to be so sure of himself. One of the things he loved most about Margot was the solid head she had on her shoulders. While he might believe he could charm any other woman into doing whatever he wanted, she had a mind of her own and wasn't afraid to use it.

And if that mind was telling her to walk away, she might actually do it no matter how great they were together.

He sat and stared at the walls, trying to figure out what would be the best move, and it kept coming back to the same thing. More time. Something he wouldn't have if he couldn't keep this contract going. And there was only one way to make sure that happened.

He picked up the phone and called his mother.

"I DON'T UNDERSTAND what the problem was."

Margot lay on the sand at Clint's favorite ocean cove, staring up at an early evening sky streaked with thin white clouds. A hundred yards from her feet, the Pacific Ocean churned in a soothing rhythm that was supposed to have calmed her nerves. Instead, the ethereal sounds of nature and the soft feel of the sand under her fingers put her in a philosophical mood, which probably wasn't the best thing given the news she'd gotten today.

"We were there," she went on. "They both had a great time. I heard Bo ask Jillian if he could call her again. She'd said yes."

"People say all kinds of things when put on the spot."

Clint was stretched out next to her propped up on one elbow, his easy expression suggesting she was making more of the situation than it warranted. But it was a big deal to Margot.

"Jillian said he'd given her tingles. Didn't she say he'd given her tingles?"

He shrugged. "I stopped trying to figure out my mother years ago. What you need to do is stop being so hard on yourself. So they slept on it and had some hesitancy about seeing each other again. It's not the end of the world."

"I know it's not the end of the world. But it doesn't make sense, either."

And it wasn't helping her confidence. Somehow, over these last several weeks, she'd completely lost her professional touch. It was as if every couple she put together ended up more wrong than right, to the extent that she now seriously doubted her future as a matchmaker. And if she couldn't make it in her chosen career, she had no idea what else she'd do.

Since high school, this had been her only plan. There hadn't been any backup ideas on what she'd do with her life. She'd structured all her schooling around counseling singles, had written her college thesis on her four core principles. She'd spent all her money and all her adult life building a career in this business.

If she wasn't any better at pairing couples than the average Joe on the street, then what was all this for?

"Margot, don't worry about it. As far as I'm concerned, you've accomplished more in two weeks than I'd ever dreamed. You got my mother to go out on a date and enjoy herself. Do you know what a feat that was?"

She frowned and watched as a seagull soared into her view, spiraling toward the earth in a slow sweep until it swirled out of her line of vision.

"It's an amazing accomplishment," he said. "And you're good at what you do. Please, don't take it personally. Mom's probably just suffering from cold feet. It's a big thing for her to venture out into the dating world after all these years. Besides, you're forgetting that neither of them said they didn't want to see each other again. They only said they wanted to think a little longer before making any more moves. Give it some time."

"I can do that."

Though she had to wonder how much time she really had in this business.

Never once had she considered the possibility of failure. Her father had never allowed that kind of thinking in the family. But with her life and her career seemingly sliding into the tank, the reality of it was knocking at her door.

The idea pricked wetness at the backs of her eyes. "I'm sorry. I'm not in a very good mood this evening. I should have turned down your offer for a walk on the beach."

He wrapped his warm hand around hers. "Nonsense. I enjoy being with you, good mood or bad."

She saw the sincerity in those sparkling blue eyes and it made her smile. As dismal as her life seemed right now, she couldn't deny that meeting Clint had been the bright spot in all of it. Aside from his obvious qualities, Margot was learning what a genuine soul lurked under that tanned and glistening skin.

He had an eerie ability to make her smile, no matter how nervous or upset she might be. They could talk about anything—news, finance and politics, even though their opinions were born from entirely opposite perspectives. He always made time for her, always looked her in the eye as if whatever she said was his most pressing issue. And when he flashed that special smile her way, her insides melted and then fluttered like ashes over a fire.

Sure, they were new. Men were always attentive when

trying to catch a woman's eye. But watching the way he interacted with his mother, Margot suspected that any woman lucky enough to catch Clint's heart would be treated with the same royalty from her first day to her last.

And when he looked at her with those smoky blue eyes, his hot hands cupping and caressing hers, and those tender lips twitching to take a taste, she couldn't help but wonder if she could really be that lucky woman.

"I don't deserve you," she said.

He responded with a slow and tender kiss to her lips.

"Of course, you deserve me."

"I need an attitude adjustment."

"You need a weekend away from it all. With me. I know a beautiful ocean side resort down in San Diego. We could leave Friday night, be down there in time for dinner." He got up and tugged her to her feet.

"A weekend away?"

"Let me pamper you for a while. We'll spend the weekend relaxing on the beach. It's got an award-winning spa, a great seafood restaurant and a swim-up bar. Or we could go to Sea World if you want some fun and frolic."

She smiled. "Fun and frolic?"

"Yeah. Fun and frolic."

Hand in hand, the two walked down to the surf and began strolling along the beach. The water chilled her toes, eroding the sand out from under her feet before slinking back into the ocean. Seagulls and black birds sparred for tidbits washed up in the surf or left behind by beachgoers. The caws and cackles mixed with the crush of the waves to produce a relaxing white noise of body and earth.

She soaked in the cool ocean air as the bright sun began to lower on the horizon, and when she did, some of the tension in her shoulders began to ease.

"I haven't been to Sea World since I was a kid."

"Then Sea World it is."

"I didn't say that. That spa thing you mentioned sounded pretty good, too."

He stopped and draped her in his arms. "We could do both. In fact, say the word and I'll cancel my appointments for the week and take you somewhere farther."

The look in his eyes said he'd actually do it, and it touched that deepest spot in her heart that he seemed to keep toying with. Oh, the life, to be able to just stop the world and take off on a few days' notice. It was more than she'd ever imagined, but though Clint might have the luxury of letting his business run itself, Margot's was currently hanging by a thread.

"At the rate I'm going, I need the appointments I've set up for next week. But I could probably swing a weekend."

He grinned as if he'd just scored the winning goal. Pulling her close, he kissed her senseless. She let her body relax against him, her soft curves filling in the spaces of his hard, muscled chest and abs. It was becoming a familiar pose, their bodies meshing together, his tongue entwined with hers, and Margot's heart racing with sensation that sped by too fast to clearly label.

Was it the silky way his lips brushed against hers? Was it the warmth that emanated from his pores? Was it the strength of his hands or his knowledge of where to put them? She only knew that when the collection came together, she lost focus. And when he was done with her, she only ached for more and more.

"It's a date, then," he said.

She smiled, thinking how perfect it was, the idea of going away and clearing her mind of all that had happened to her lately. And for the second time in two weeks, she found herself thankful for Clint and his knight-in-shining-armor timing. Somehow, the man had perfected the art of whisking in and giving her exactly what she needed when she needed it. And she wasn't going to question what it meant or where they were going. For now, she would simply be thankful she had him on her side.

14

"Margot agreed to go to San Diego with me this weekend."

Clint gave his mother a peck on the cheek before he dropped his laptop on the counter and poured himself a cup of coffee. Lately, his mom had taken up the habit of rising early and chatting with him before work, and he had to admit he appreciated the gesture. Maybe it was because Margot had made them a threesome, helping take some of the weight of entertaining her off his shoulders. Or maybe, thanks to Margot, he'd simply been in a better mood in general. Either way, his life was improving since she'd become a part of it. Now he just needed to make sure it stayed that way.

"Thank heaven for small favors," Jillian said. She took a bite from her bowl of fresh fruit while browsing the entertainment section of the *Los Angeles Times*. "Really, Clint, I never would have gone along with your idea if I'd known she'd react the way she did. The poor woman was devastated when she thought I wasn't interested in Bo."

"Mom, all you were supposed to do was tell her you wanted to take a few more days to think about it before committing to seeing him again. You and Bo weren't supposed to go into cahoots and *both* back out on it."

"I couldn't let Bo think that was true. I had to call and give him the heads-up, and when I did he offered to play along. It's not my fault he went overboard." She pointed a finger.

"This is the problem with lies. They're never simple. You've got to tell a second one to cover the first and a third to cover the second and before long, you've got too many people involved and you're in over your head."

He rolled his eyes. "Between you and Margot, this whole thing has been blown out of proportion. Must women always be so dramatic?"

"Can't men just tell women the truth?"

"It was one tiny white lie, and after this weekend, everything will be on the table."

"Really," she said skeptically.

"Yep. I've got it all planned out. I'm treating Margot to the best weekend of her life. We'll spend Friday and Saturday at the resort, then I got Bob Anway to lend me his yacht Sunday. It'll be a weekend of luxury, and by the time we get back, she'll understand in no uncertain terms how serious I am about her. Just give me this trip to get her on board and then you and Bo can see as much of each other as you want."

"Would you listen to yourself? You make this sound like it's another one of your business deals."

In a tactical way, it was. After all, what was Clint's job other than to woo people into putting their faith in him? And it was a job he did well. So why not use those same talents to get Margot to give up this idea of breaking things off once their contract was satisfied.

Starting Friday night, he intended to show her a weekend like she'd never dreamed, pulling out all the stops and leaving every base covered. He'd treat her to a weekend of luxury and lovemaking, showing her in words and action that he was serious about their relationship and he wanted her to be serious about it, too.

And he had every confidence it would work. Why shouldn't it? Attracting females was one of his better skills.

If it hadn't been for this Rob guy messing her up like he had, Margot would have already been reeled in by now. But that was okay. So he had to work a bit harder. No one ever accused him of walking away from a challenge. In fact, he lived for them. And this weekend, he'd demonstrate just how good he was at getting what he wanted when he set his mind to it.

"In case you haven't noticed," he replied, "the business is doing pretty well, Mom."

"I hope you know what you're doing. I certainly didn't like the tone in her voice yesterday when I told her I wanted to think about Bo before making any more dates. She was shocked and confused. And I don't blame her. After the way I'd gushed about him, she probably thinks I'm a fruitcake, backing down the next day."

"I promise she won't think you're a fruitcake by Monday." He took her empty bowl and rinsed it in the sink. "I only need this weekend, Mom. After that, there won't be any more white lies. You can see Bo all you want."

"Actually, I'm seeing him Friday."

He looked up to see a wide grin on her face. "Friday?"

"Yes, when I talked to him we made lunch plans." Then she shrugged. "I only promised to keep it from Margot. I never promised not to see Bo again."

Clint thought it over and couldn't come up with anything wrong with that. After all, this had all been about setting his mother up with a new social life, and he did genuinely like Bo Granger.

And he also wasn't lying about all the deception being over and done with this weekend. To be honest, Clint hadn't expected Margot to react the way she had, either. She'd been so lost and disillusioned last night, he'd nearly confessed right there on the beach. He hadn't thought she would have been so upset over his mom and Bo wanting to think things over before setting another date. In retrospect, if given the opportunity to do it over again, he probably would have come up with another plan.

But he'd managed to lift Margot's spirits, and by the time the night had been through, he'd convinced himself that one or two days of disappointment on her part was worth the ultimate cause. He wanted her in his life. If he had to pull a few extra strings to get that to happen, he'd have to live with that.

"Just make sure you don't run into Margot together," he warned.

"Clint, the two of you are leaving for the weekend. And you promised me next week the farce is over." She stood and tightened the belt on her robe. "I'm serious. I'm putting my foot down after this weekend. She either wants to keep dating you or she doesn't, and if she comes back still hesitant about getting involved, you need to respect that and back off. Contrary to your belief, you don't always get what you want when you want it."

He smiled. "Yes, actually, I do."

She narrowed her eyes at him, knowing he was right.

"You can't force her to love you on your schedule."

No, but he could keep her from running away from it. One of the things that drove Clint so mad about the situation was that as often as he saw that small flicker of fear in her eyes, he also saw the warmth of something deep. If it hadn't been for the trouble she'd been through lately, he knew Margot would be in the same place he was right now, admitting to herself that there was something strong between them they needed to keep pursuing. If this had been a matter of a woman uninterested, he would have given up a long time ago. But he knew that wasn't the case. Margot wanted him as badly as he wanted her. She just needed some serious coaxing to look over that wall of hers and see it. And this weekend, he intended to treat her to such a display of wealth and attention that she wouldn't dream of walking away.

"I only have to get her to see what's already in her heart, Mom. That's all I've got to do."

"You make it sound so simple."

It was simple. He was Clint Hilton, after all.

MARGOT CHECKED her watch. Only four hours and thirty-seven minutes before Clint picked her up at her condo and they were off to San Diego for the weekend. She couldn't wait. It had been a long and difficult week, worsened by the fact that Alan and Gene had taken an early summer vacation to attend Gene's sister's wedding up in North Dakota. Not only could Margot have used Alan's professional support these last few days, but the office had been too quiet without him.

This was not a good time for her to be left alone with her thoughts. Since talking to Bo and Jillian this week, her professional outlook had soured to the point where she was teetering on depression. Her mental glass was half-empty, the bright side eclipsed by her bad mood and ever growing self-doubt. It wasn't the best place to be in, and she found herself watching the clock, waiting for this last appointment so she could go home, pack and be ready when Clint came to take her the heck out of here for a couple days.

The sound of the front door opening perked her mood and she rose from her desk to go greet Stacy. It had been a couple weeks since she'd sent Stacy off with a laundry list of things to do. First and foremost had been to make an appointment with Margot's business associate, Claire, a woman who worked at Macy's and provided free consultation on clothing and makeup. Margot hoped Claire was able to talk Stacy out of her short skirts and skimpy tops, show her how to lighten up her makeup and tone down her pretty blond hair. Margot had also told Stacy to stop going to the tanning booths, and by now, some of the overt color on her skin should have faded.

Anxious to see the result, Margot stepped out of her office and down the short hall, and when she caught sight of her new client, she was shocked.

The woman hadn't changed a thing.

"Stacy," she said, eyeing her from the top of her teased-up ponytail down to toes polished a shiny apple-green color. Not to mention all the bare skin in between.

Stacy had traded in the miniskirt for a pair of short jean shorts, a neon-green bikini top and a trendy undersized jacket that barely cleared her breasts. The color scheme seemed to be green today, which would have pleasantly matched her eyes if only one could get close enough to see past the mascara.

Stunned and disappointed, Margot asked, "Did you…uh… meet with Claire?"

Stacy was grinning from ear to ear, nearly bursting with excitement over something, and Margot tried to imagine what it was. She prayed it wasn't pride in her "transformation," since Margot couldn't make out the slightest change other than a color shift from hot pink to tangy green.

"No," Stacy said, beaming. "I found a man."

"You found…okay." She gestured toward the hall. "Why don't you come back and tell me about him."

"Oh, he's amazing," Stacy gushed as they stepped into Margot's office and took their seats. "He's this guy who's been coming to the bar for, like, ever. I never thought he was all that cute so I didn't pay much attention to him. But a couple weeks ago—two days after I saw you, actually—he asked me out, and I was in such a bad mood about men that I told him sure, but he's not getting any, so if he thinks I'm going to put out, he's wasting his time. And you know what he said?"

Margot shook her head.

"He said that was fine, and then he took me out to *dinner,* and when we got home, he kissed me goodbye, asked if he could see me again and went home. Is that the most awesome thing ever?"

"Um…yeah."

For the next ten minutes, Stacy rattled on about Drake, her new boyfriend, and the dates they'd gone on. The woman was so thrilled, she chattered a mile a minute, and the more she talked, the more Margot wondered why she'd kept their appointment. It sounded as if Stacy had found her Prince Charming, which was usually the point when Margot's business with her clients ended.

"And when we finally did have sex," Stacy went on, "he ended up being totally amazing in bed. Isn't that funny? Here's a guy I'd barely noticed who comes along when I'm ready to give up on great sex and he ends up being the best I've ever had!"

"That's…great."

Margot wasn't sure what else she was supposed to say. If Stacy had come seeking advice, she hadn't said so.

"And you know what the best thing of all is?" Stacy asked. "He likes me exactly the way I am. He doesn't want me to change a thing. Not my hair, my clothes, not anything."

Margot took a deep breath and blinked. "I think that's great, Stacy. It sounds like you've found a man who's perfect for you."

"Yeah." Stacy finally sobered her expression. "And, well, obviously he doesn't want me seeing *you* anymore."

"Of course," Margot said, pasting a fake smile on her face.

Stacy pulled out her checkbook. "But you were so nice and sweet that I didn't want to just not show up or cop out and leave a voice mail message or something. Besides, you people usually have a fee for not canceling twenty-four hours in advance, don't you? I've been so busy this week, I forgot until this morning."

She ground her teeth. "No, actually I don't."

"Oh. Well, are you sure? I mean, Drake offered to pay." She grinned and giggled. "Isn't that sweet?"

Margot held on to the smile. "That's very sweet, but no, you don't owe me a thing. My initial consultation is always free and you don't need to pay if you've chosen not to use my services. I'm just happy you've found someone who seems to really care for you. That's the important thing."

Stacy tucked her checkbook back in her purse and stood. "Oh, you are *so* nice. At the very least, I'll make sure to tell all my single friends about you."

"That would be nice. Thanks."

Margot followed her out of the office, said her goodbyes and tried to swallow down the lump in her throat as she watched Stacy skip away. Margot wasn't upset over losing the client. Heck, she'd only half expected Stacy to show up in the first place, feeling from their first meeting that Stacy hadn't been crazy about Margot's suggestions. No, what got to Margot was that it had happened *today,* as the proverbial capper to a horrible week, when she'd already been carrying around a heavy load of self-doubt and could have used a tiny nugget of something positive to leave with.

Instead, what she got was another client saying thanks but no thanks, and it wasn't what she needed right now.

Margot turned back to her office and dropped to her seat. Oh, what was happening to her? With every day that passed her confidence kept sliding farther into the toilet. In a situation like this, the old Margot would have never just sat there and let Stacy walk out the door. At the very least, Margot would have asked Stacy some questions about this new relationship, engaged her in an exploratory discussion and maybe offered some parting advice. Margot's philosophy had always been that each and every client taught her something, and she might have garnered additional insights from Stacy had she pulled herself together enough to keep her business hat on.

When in fact, she'd just sat there and taken the whole thing as a personal blow, much like she had when she'd spoken to Jillian and Bo earlier in the week.

Margot still couldn't grasp what had gone wrong with those two, and the fact that she hadn't prodded for more answers showed just how lost she'd become. Two months ago, she would have used their experience to get better acquainted with their preferences. Bad dates happened all the time and were supposed to be part of the investigative process between her and her clients. Before all these problems had derailed her, her take-charge attitude would have kicked in, she would have pulled out a pad and pen and started taking notes instead of sitting there feeling as if the world were conspiring against her. So what happened to throw her this far off balance? And more importantly, how could she get her life back on track again?

She thought of what her father would say if he saw her sitting there in her office on the verge of pity tears. No doubt, something about his days in Vietnam, how he didn't have time to feel sorry for himself when he was dodging bullets in the jungle.

Try watching your best friend get his head blown off three feet from where you're standing. That's something to ruin your day. Everything short of that is a picnic.

All their lives, Margot and her siblings had rolled their eyes or affectionately mimicked their father's wartime anecdotes. So it came as a surprise to her how often she reflected on them for strength now that her parents had moved out of state and she was on her own. It didn't take much guesswork to know how her dad would react to the idea that she'd let a few personal and professional setbacks get her down. He'd tell her that nothing got accomplished by sitting around feeling sorry for herself. That what she needed to do was pull it together and get to work fixing her problems.

Which, at this moment, meant getting back with Bo and Jillian and finding out exactly what went wrong with their date. Maybe it was like Clint said. Maybe Jillian simply got cold feet and felt things were moving too fast. Maybe there was something about Bo she didn't like and wasn't confessing. Either way, Margot couldn't help if she didn't understand her clients, and Jillian and Bo were missed opportunities she'd let her emotions get in the way of.

She reached for the phone, intending to call Jillian and ask more questions, but decided things like this were better handled in person. Checking her watch, she saw that she had plenty of time to drop by Clint's for a chat, so without wasting another minute, she grabbed her purse and locked up for the weekend.

She used the twenty-minute drive to formulate her questions, recognizing that she'd have to shift her usual tactics given that Jillian technically wasn't a regular client. She'd have to approach the woman as a friend and play it more subtly, but that was okay. The goal was the same. It was only the method of getting there that would need some shifting.

By the time she turned up Clint's street, she'd come up with a pretty solid plan of action. All of which slipped from her mind when she neared Clint's house and found Bo's car parked in the driveway.

For a long moment, she sat in her car on the quiet street and stared at the black Jaguar parked in Clint's spot. Her first thought was that she'd been mistaken, that it was someone else's car, but the personalized license plate left no doubts. It was Bo Granger. And what he was doing at Clint's house, she had no idea.

She pulled into the driveway and stepped out of the car, using the short walk to contemplate a reasonable explanation. Was he returning something Jillian had left behind at the restaurant? That could be. Though no one had mentioned it in the week since their date.

She rapped on the door and then rang the doorbell, prompting Pom Pom into a barking frenzy on the other side that didn't let up until Jillian answered the door. And when she did, the shock in her eyes gave Margot more questions than answers.

"Margot! Wha—what are you doing here?"

Margot peeked over the woman's shoulder into the great room that spanned through to the back of the house. "Is Bo here?"

Jillian touched a hand to her throat. "Um…"

Just then, Margot spotted Bo stepping through the patio doors, a martini glass in his hand and a wide grin on his face.

A grin that disappeared fast once he made eye contact with Margot.

She looked at Jillian, then back at Bo. "What's going on?"

Jillian stuttered before finally frowning in a huff. "Oh, I *told* Clint this was a bad idea."

"*What* was a bad idea?"

Stepping back, Jillian held out a hand. "Why don't you come in?"

15

"WHAT DO YOU *mean* you had to tell her the truth?"

Clint held his cell phone to his ear as he shut the door to his office and took a seat behind his desk.

"Obviously, I never expected her to drop by out of the blue," his mother explained. "She caught Bo and me completely off guard."

"So you told her *everything?*"

"I had no choice. Margot's not stupid," she said, clearly exasperated. "This is exactly why I don't approve of things like this. The truth always comes out, and now Bo and I feel terrible and Margot's upset."

Oh, great.

He placed a hand to his forehead. "Is she still there? Let me talk to her."

"No, she stormed out of here. She's not happy with you— or any of us, for that matter. You know how distraught she was when she thought I wasn't interested in Bo. Now she's doubly upset to find out we'd all lied to her."

Great, just great. Why couldn't things have gone his way for three more measly hours? Three hours. That was all he'd needed, but for some reason lately, when it came to his love life, his mother's timing continually sucked. Nevertheless, he knew this was his fault and didn't need his mother reminding him of that.

"You should call her. You need to apologize."

"I know." He only hoped it would be that simple. "Did she say where she was going?"

"Home, I assume. You two are taking off for the weekend, though judging by the angry way she left, I wouldn't count on that anymore."

"She was that mad?"

"She certainly didn't leave here smiling. Poor Bo feels horrible. Margot is a friend of his daughter, you know."

"I'll call you back later," he said.

He hung up then dialed Margot's number, disappointed but not surprised when she didn't answer. Apparently, she didn't want to talk to him right now, and he wondered how bad a sign that was. He supposed it was better than having her pick up and scream, "You bastard!"

Or was it?

When he got her voice mail, he left a message. Then he picked up a set of revised plans for the Proctor house and walked them out to Carmen's desk.

"Margot hasn't called in the last half hour or so, has she?"

Carmen shook her head. "No, why?"

"Just wondering," he mumbled. "Where's Brad?"

"At the post office. He should be back any minute."

He set the package on Carmen's desk. "When he gets back, have him take these up to the Proctor house. They're the revised plans, and Stan is waiting for them. I was going to take them myself but something's come up."

"No problem."

Without another word, he ducked out the door and headed for Margot's, using the ten-minute drive to mentally slap himself. This should have never happened. He should have known better than to conspire behind Margot's back, but for some reason, his judgment had taken leave and he wasn't sure why.

He pulled up to her condo, pleased to see her car parked in her spot. It was only when he got to the door and rang the bell that it occurred to him he had no idea what to say. Ironic, since all morning he'd been mentally reciting the speech he intended to give her this weekend, the one where he shared his feelings, opened his heart and coaxed her into giving their relationship a serious shot.

Now he'd have some backpedaling to do before he could get them to that point.

When she didn't answer, he rang again, then knocked. "Margot, it's Clint. Please let me in."

Eventually the dead bolt turned, and she opened the door, her expression telling him he had more than backpedaling to do. There would probably be some groveling involved, too. Because inside those big brown eyes were some pretty angry flames.

"Let me explain," he urged as he stepped inside and closed the door behind him.

He walked past the small entry and into her living room, brushing a hand through his hair while he tried to come up with the right words to start. But before he could open his mouth, she spoke out in an accusing tone that confirmed how much trouble he was in.

"You made me think Bo and Jillian weren't interested in each other."

"Now, that's not exactly true—"

"You knew how much that hurt me, yet you let me think it anyway."

"It was a bad idea, I know."

She squeezed her hands into fists as her eyes began to shimmer with tears, and Clint wished he could rewind the clock and do this last week over again. He hated seeing her upset like this, the hurt and frustration, and it struck a blade through his conscience.

"You knew how much trouble I've been having at work lately," she added. "And you deliberately made it worse."

"I didn't—okay, maybe—"

Then those angry eyes went wide with bewilderment, "*Why?* Why would you do such a thing?"

"I—I didn't want you to break things off."

The words sounded small and idiotic once he said them, which only underscored the stupidity of what he'd done. And it was then that he stopped to wonder what had been driving his actions these last couple of weeks.

What had happened to the take-them-or-leave-them guy who never let a woman swallow up his self-confidence? Where was the man who'd never let relationships get serious enough for problems like this? Where had his sensibility gone? And why was he now standing there so desperately afraid of the look on this woman's face?

He knew the answer to all those questions. Every one of them trailed back to one thing.

Somewhere along the line, he'd fallen in love with Margot Roth.

It was a revelation that both thrilled and terrified him. Through his adult life, he hadn't thought much about love. He only knew someday that it would in the end find him. And now that it had, he couldn't shake off the elation of having something so precious within his grasp, of looking at this beautiful woman and knowing she was the one he wanted to spend the rest of his life with.

But along with it came the fear of losing what he'd found. And it was that fear, the newness of it all and his inexperience in dealing with it that had been driving his actions. He'd been half-crazy lately because for the first time ever, he'd found something worth fighting for. And the idea of losing wasn't an option he would consider.

"You weren't ready to end this fling," she said. "So you decided you'd rather let me think I'd failed?"

"I told you before, this isn't a fling."

"It's not a relationship, either."

"I'd like it to be." He stepped forward and tried to touch her, but she backed away.

"You don't get it." She held up four fingers. "The four principles—friendship, respect, *honest communication,* common ground—*that's* a relationship."

"You forgot to mention love."

She blinked and opened her mouth, ready to make a comeback before apparently realizing she didn't have one.

"Margot," he urged. "I'm sorry. What I did was stupid and wrong. Let me make it up to you. Let's go to San Diego and get away from everything for a couple days. I've got an amazing weekend planned. We've got reservations at the best resort, a private yacht for sailing Sunday—"

"You think those kinds of things matter to me?" She shook her head. "This whole thing, it isn't right."

"I know and I'm sorry for lying to you."

"No." She waved a finger between them. "I'm talking about you and me. What we've been doing isn't right. It hasn't been from the start."

He swallowed. "I disagree."

"How can you say that? We come from completely different worlds. We don't share the same values."

"What values don't we share?"

"*Honesty,* for one."

He closed his eyes and sighed. "Okay, I deserved that. But the man you've seen this week isn't who I am. I *am* honest. And so what if we come from different places? We're here now, and I think we're good together."

Closing the gap between them, he softened his tone and

cradled her cheek in his hand, tilting her chin to look her squarely in the eye. "I'm in love with you, Margot. And I don't care to make sense of it. I only know how I feel." He took her hand and placed it against his racing heart. "This tells me what we have is right. It's all I need."

MARGOT STOOD and stared, frozen by Clint's words and not entirely convinced she'd heard them correctly.

He loved her? She had no idea what to do with that, and certainly wasn't prepared to respond. Like he'd been doing since the day they'd met, he'd managed to twist her thoughts full circle to the point where she didn't know who she was or where she was going.

Half of her wanted to jump into his arms and squeal with delight, thrilled that this handsome and powerful man cared so deeply about her. And that only proved how senseless she'd become, because everything about their affair screamed danger. And if she hadn't heard it before, his profession of love yelled it loud and clear. She wasn't ready for a new relationship, especially one moving this fast. It was too much too soon, and she looked at him with apologetic eyes and backed from his grasp. "I'm not ready for that at all."

"You don't need to be ready. Let's keep going as we have and see where this goes. Just—" he reached out and touched her arm "—just don't walk away from us."

A chill of dread came over her, and she circled her arms around her waist. She didn't know what to do with this. Disillusionment and uncertainty consumed her to the point where she felt paralyzed with fear. It seemed as if these last four weeks had been one giant practical joke, where all her beliefs and expectations had been turned on end and the only thing left was the big "Gotcha!"

Except it wasn't a joke. It was her life. And the big "Gotcha!" was a rich and sexy playboy professing his love.

There were so many things wrong with this picture she didn't know where to begin. But she knew one thing for sure—maintaining the status quo wouldn't help straighten out her head or her career.

Slowly, she turned to look him square in the eye. "I'm sorry, but I can't do this anymore."

"I'm not asking you to marry me. I'm only asking that we keep things going and that you keep an open mind."

"But that's the problem. I don't know where my mind is at. I haven't since the day you walked into my office."

He smiled assuredly. "Hon, you're going through a rough patch professionally, and I haven't helped. Half of it is my fault, and I'm sorry. But if you'll let me make it up to you, I'll show you that we can work through this together."

They were nice words, the kind of words she would have expected from a lover and life partner. And she'd love to accept them. But she knew in her heart, her problems weren't being helped by this whirlwind romance. She couldn't sort things out while she was spending every evening in this fantasy castle Clint was building around them.

Feeling weak, she moved to the dining table and sat down. "We can't work it out together. I need to do it on my own."

"Margot, a few hours ago we were planning a break from here. Go with me to San Diego. It will be good for you. We'll relax, catch up on sleep, walk on the beach and talk things through. I know with some time away, you'll see things more clearly and—"

"Stop! Please, just stop." She placed her head in her hands. "A weekend in a resort isn't the answer. Neither is a shopping trip or a fancy dinner. What I need is some space, and I haven't had a moment of that since I came home from Rob's and found you standing at my doorstep."

"Fine." His voice was tinged with a touch of annoyance, though she knew he was trying hard to hide it. "I'll give you space."

"Clint, I need more space than you think, more than you're willing to give."

"I'll give you whatever you need, Margot. If you'll only promise me that you'll give us a try once you've figured out what it is you have to figure out."

"I'm sorry, I can't make a promise like that." While she knew he was trying to be kind and supportive and wonderful, it only felt to her as if she was being backed into a corner.

Fifteen minutes ago, she'd been furious, a day before that she'd been forlorn, and before that she'd been hurt and dismayed. In the last few weeks, she'd gone from elation to devastation and back again more times than she could count, all thanks to the men in her life.

It had to stop.

"I don't know what's in my heart, and I don't know how long it will take me to put my life back in order." Then she paused and blinked back a swell of tears. "And I can't promise you we can simply pick up where we left off. I need a break. I need a long, thorough break."

He stood with his hands fisted at his sides, the casual ease in his jaw now tightened, and the warm look in his eyes now chilled. "So that's it. I tell you I love you and you tell me no thanks. Not now, not ever."

The pain in his voice stung deep. "I need space," she choked out. "I need time to myself to try and figure this out."

For a long moment he stood there, his only movement the grinding of his teeth as he studied her. She didn't know what he was calculating in that head, and she definitely didn't want to think of how badly her words might have hurt him. But they'd needed to be said. At this point in her life, the only thing she was sure of was her desperate need to retreat and regroup. Without that, she was only prolonging the inevitable, and though it didn't seem like it right now, she knew it would be worse if she let it go on.

He stepped to her and clasped her hand in his, looking down at her fingers and covering them in warmth. "I need one honest answer from you." He met her gaze. "Do you have feelings for me at all?"

The need in his eyes unnerved her, and though she questioned if it was best, she had no choice but to answer him honestly. "Yes, I do."

He seemed to be reading her gaze, as if to confirm her words were true. He nodded. "Then I'll wait while you figure out what I already know."

"Clint, please."

He touched his fingers to her lips. "You take your break. And when you realize how much you love me, I'll be waiting for you."

She opened her mouth to argue, but before a word could spill out, he took her in his arms and covered her mouth with his.

Raw sorrow had her sinking against him and clinging to his chest as if this were the last kiss they'd share. Because no matter what he said, she knew it was. Her problems weren't going to be worked out in a day or two, and despite what he might say, she knew the man she was dealing with.

He might truly believe in their relationship, might even believe he really loved her. But he wasn't the type to keep pining away at a lost romance, nor was he one to put his life on hold waiting for her to come around. So with the finality of the occasion weighing heavily on her, she pressed into the kiss and took the last he had to offer.

She breathed heavily to soak in his scent and brushed her fingers over his chest, following every muscle and curve so that she could retrace them in her mind. She caressed her tongue around his, tasting the sweet essence of his lips, filling all her senses and tucking them away for safekeeping.

And when they were done, he squeezed her hand and said again, "Come get me when you're ready."

Then he stepped to the door and walked out. And though Margot would have liked to believe otherwise, she knew in her heart that was probably the last she would ever see of Clint Hilton.

16

"MY GUESS is you probably won't lose any money in this, but you won't have made any once the contract is terminated."

Clint listened to the advice of his lawyer, Dwayne Montgomery, over the phone while staring out the windows of his office.

"Proctor is playing hardball with a few clauses," Dwayne went on. "I don't think he's got a leg to stand on, but the fight alone could cost more than it's worth."

"Let's cut our losses and get out," Clint said. "I want this contract over as much as he does, so as long as it doesn't cost me a fortune, I'm willing to bend."

"Good enough. I'll work up a settlement recommendation and get back to you."

"Thanks, Dwayne." He disconnected the call then turned to find his mother standing in the doorway.

"Mom. What brings you downtown?"

"Lunch with Bo." She stepped into his office and set her purse on the conference table. "It's been a long time since I've seen Carmen and I thought I'd stop by and say hi."

He crossed the room and kissed her on the cheek. "It's a nice surprise. You don't come around here as much as you used to."

"Well, you know." She shrugged, looking around the room that had been her husband's office for more than twenty-five years.

Like the house she'd sold, this office held too many ghosts of Jerry Hilton, and since his death, Clint's mother hadn't cared to spend much time there. Though Clint suspected her new relationship with Bo was doing wonders where that was concerned.

In the few weeks that Bo and Jillian had been dating, Clint had noticed a distinct change in his mother. Or, more accurately, he noticed her returning to the woman she'd been before they lost his dad. Much of her confidence was back, along with her sense of humor. And she'd started seeing some of her old friends again, people she'd gradually shied away from because after being half of a couple for so many years, she wasn't sure how to deal with them as a single woman. But with a new love life to talk about, Clint noticed Jillian reacquainting herself with several longtime friends. There had even been rumors of a reconciliation with Marge, though he'd believe that one when he saw it.

It looked as though when it came to his contract with Margot, she'd delivered more than he'd dreamed. He only wished their personal matters had ended up so well.

He was nearing the one-month mark since he'd walked out of her condo, and in all that time, he hadn't heard a peep. With every new day that passed, his confidence in their relationship went farther and farther in the tank. He had to admit that when he'd walked out that night, he'd been certain Margot would call in a day or two, a week tops. After all, Clint didn't go around telling every woman he dated that he loved her. In fact, Margot had been the one and only.

He'd assumed that meant as much to her as it did to him. Apparently, he was wrong. And despite Carmen's assurances that Margot cared deeply for him, he wasn't sure how much longer he could sit around and wait for her to sort out her feelings. While Clint had a number of good qualities, patience wasn't one of them. His only dilemma at this point was whether he should storm over to her office and make another valiant effort, or consider his first love lost—neither option very promising.

"Was that Dwayne Montgomery on the phone?" Jillian asked.

"Yes." Clint rubbed the back of his neck and tucked his phone in his pocket. "The company is officially parting ways with the Proctors."

"What do you mean by parting ways?"

He stepped over to the conference table and took a seat. Over the last year, he'd talked less and less about work with his mom, sensing her desire to start putting that part of her life behind her. And while it had been good for her, Clint had suffered. It had already been hard losing his dad, who'd been as much a friend and mentor as a father figure to him. Having his mom back away and leave the business in his hands, while flattering, had left a hole where his support system used to be.

Case in point, the Proctor fiasco.

"They've canceled construction on their beach home and want to get out from under it. I'd consider buying the house myself and finishing it on spec, but I've had so much trouble with those people, I just want to get out of it, too."

She reacted with surprise. "Why are they selling? Did they run out of money?"

Clint shook his head. "No, they've got plenty of money. The problem is that intern I've got, Ed Mahoney's grandson, Brad. I'd sent the kid over there to deliver some plans to Stan and he ran into Proctor himself. I'm still not clear what the hell he did, but somehow the kid struck up a conversation and ended up selling Proctor on some resort property down around Mexico. Now Proctor's sold on Central America, wants out from under his Malibu home, and we're screwed."

Clint still couldn't believe it. Every time he told the story, it sounded more and more incredulous. Proctor's favorite motto had always been never trust anyone under thirty, yet give the man ten minutes with a half-witted beach bum and suddenly he's putting his house on the market and buying vacation property in a country that doesn't even speak his language.

Jillian shook her head. "When you deal with people like the Proctors, things like this are bound to happen."

It was her way of reminding him that his father would have never bid on that job, and Clint didn't miss the jab. But before his annoyance could set in she placed a hand over his and smiled warmly. "Some things you need to learn on your own. Your father made his mistakes along the way, and you'll make them, too. And just like he did, you'll benefit from the experience and move on."

He curled his fingers around hers and gave them a light squeeze. "I miss him."

"You two were close. In some ways even closer than he and I were."

It was true. Clint had always been his father's son, and when the man died, Clint lost more than just his dad. He'd lost his best friend and confidant. It wasn't something he dwelled on often. These last two years, he'd been so busy keeping the business together and then supporting his mother he'd never had the luxury of feeling the weight of his own loss. But in times like this, the hole his father left behind seemed wide and bottomless, even more prominent lately because, for a short while, Margot had managed to fill some of it.

He missed being able to relax after work and share the details of his day with someone who understood. He'd liked talking with her about the business, bouncing ideas off her and getting her take on things. Margot had a solid sensibility, and he'd quickly found that her conservative outlook nicely tempered his idealistic tendencies. She'd given him back that counterbalance he'd lost when his father died, which made it hurt all the more to lose that support a second time.

"I hope you're keeping Ed's grandson away from the clients from now on," she said.

Clint took a long breath and groaned. "I'd like to lose him for good. He's been nothing but trouble, and I've got another six weeks before he's going back to school."

"So, what can you do?"

"I don't know. If I'd listened to Margot, I wouldn't still be dealing with him now. She'd told me right off I needed to have a heart-to-heart with Edward about him, but I didn't want to offend one of Dad's oldest friends."

She perked. "You've talked to Margot?"

"No. That conversation was a month ago. I still haven't heard a word." Then he gave his mom a sideways glance. "You?"

"No. But I'm very proud of you for respecting her needs. I didn't think you had it in you."

"Gee, thanks."

"Don't be offended. It's a trait you share with your father. Neither of you were ever one to sit back and let things take their own course. You work on your time schedule and no one else's." She patted his hand. "But I think this is good for you, learning to wait for the things you want."

"Yeah, well, my patience is running out. At some point I have to accept the idea that some things aren't meant to be."

"Some things aren't meant to be *controlled,* you mean. Trust me, Margot won't be led around on a leash. If you two are going to have a successful future it's best you learn to live with that now. You did a good thing backing off and giving her space when she asked. And you've done a remarkable job keeping your word. Give her more time. She'll come around."

He wished he shared his mother's optimism. Unfortunately, the more time that passed, the less certain Clint was that he had a future with Margot. And as they neared the one-month mark since that night he'd walked away, he began to face a reality he hadn't allowed himself to consider before. That to save his own sanity, he might really have to cut his losses and move on.

"Was that David I just saw leaving?" Alan asked, glancing down the hall from the doorway of Margot's office.

"Yes," she said. "He stopped in to tell me he won't be needing my services anymore."

David was Margot's latest client lost, though at least this time it wasn't because she hadn't done her job. "He's in love. With a man. One of the friends he went to Cabo San Lucas with, apparently."

Alan leaned against the doorjamb and folded his arms over his chest. "Yup, we both saw that coming."

"I suppose."

He gave her a scolding look. "Would you cheer up? You've been moping around here for weeks. David was a success. He came here seeking your help and you did exactly what he needed you to do. He's a case you should be proud of."

She smiled, appreciating what her partner was trying to do, but it did little to lift her spirits.

These last few weeks had been some of her most difficult, and through all the pain and effort, she was no closer to finding any answers. She'd been spending most of her spare time going over recent client files hoping to find some clue as to what was going wrong with her career. What she found was that it didn't simply *seem* as though she'd been on a bad streak lately—she really *was*. And the worst of it was that she couldn't clearly see the problem.

"It's not David. It's all my clients lately. I'm losing my touch, Alan." And what she didn't say was that she was scared to death, not to mention depressed.

She'd sacrificed her love life, believing that if she'd only separated herself from all distraction then she could figure out what was going wrong with her career. That somehow, magically, the answers would present themselves. But here she was, almost four weeks later, with nothing more than a broken heart.

The truth was, while she could remove Clint from her physical life, she couldn't remove him from her heart or her thoughts. Instead of stepping away and gaining clarity, all she'd done was grow more and more confused.

"You aren't losing your touch," Alan said. "What you are is too hard on yourself. You expect perfection, and you've got to remember this is an imperfect science. You're going to have clients you don't connect with, people you can't help. And I've learned after more than a decade in this business that, I don't know why, they always come in clumps. What you can't do is lose your confidence because of it."

Margot had to admit that's exactly what had happened. She'd gone through a rough streak and it seemed ever since then, the seed of doubt was planted and growing. Little by little, she'd gone farther off track to the point where now everything she touched seemed to blow up in her face.

"You're doing fine, Margot, really. You just need to ride out the storm."

Forcing a smile, she thanked him, wishing she could believe his words, but falling short. At this point, she needed more than assurance to get her out of her slump. She needed answers.

He looked at his watch. "I've got a late lunch with a client, but I'll be back in a few hours. Why don't we do happy hour at Rigley's? I can't remember the last time we went for drinks."

She smiled. "I'd love that."

"It's a date," he said. "I'll be back around four." When she nodded, he pulled his keys from his pocket and made his way out.

She really did need to get out of this office and take in a change of scenery, even though she knew Alan would only use the time to tell her to stop worrying. It was what he'd been doing ever since he and Gene got back from North Dakota. She supposed the reassurance didn't hurt. Left unchecked, she might have allowed her fear and doubt to completely consume her. But on the other hand, she wished there were someone out there who could point to what was going wrong with her life and tell her how to fix it.

We can work through this together.

Clint's words haunted her, especially during times such as this when she felt afraid and alone. Several times a day lately, she'd stared at the phone, begging herself to pick it up and dial his number. Four weeks ago, she hadn't understood how badly she would miss him, and instead of her yearning easing with time, it only seemed to get stronger.

Though Carmen had told her he was still waiting patiently, Margot had trouble believing it. Not that she thought Carmen would lie, but she doubted the woman knew all the comings and goings of her boss. And if she didn't, Margot wasn't certain she could handle that call. It already hurt enough thinking he might have gone on with his love life. She couldn't handle having him verify it. It was better imagining him still waiting for her than face the crush that she'd blown yet another aspect of her life.

Because no matter how often her head told her she'd done the right thing in pushing him away, her heart kept insisting she'd made the biggest mistake of her life.

The opening of the front door pulled her from her thoughts, and she called out, "What happened? You forget something?"

Expecting to see Alan, she was startled when she heard Jillian's voice. "Hello?"

"Jillian?" She rose from her chair and began to round her desk when Clint's mother stepped to her doorway.

"I haven't come at a bad time, have I?" Jillian asked, looking hesitantly around Margot's office.

"No. I don't have an appointment for about an hour." She stepped over and gave Jillian a warm hug. Though Margot had spoken with Jillian on the phone a few times over the last few weeks, seeing her in person reminded Margot that along with Clint, she'd missed them both desperately. "Please sit down. Can I offer you some coffee?"

Jillian waved it away. "No, thank you. I'd had lunch with Bo earlier today and your name came up. We remembered that neither of us has checked in with you lately, so I thought I'd stop by."

"Things are still going well?"

"Wonderfully." Jillian smiled with a light in her eyes Margot had never seen before. There was a new freshness about her, a special perk Margot often saw in clients who were experiencing the joys of a budding new relationship. It was the best part of Margot's job, witnessing that transformation, and it thrilled her to see that success with Jillian, for both their sakes.

"You know," Jillian said, "after Jerry, I never thought another man could make me happy, but you proved me wrong with Bo. Every day, I've got to pinch myself to believe it's real."

"I'm so glad."

Margot listened eagerly while Jillian recounted the things

she and Bo had done since they last spoke, places they'd gone, other couples they'd started seeing socially.

"I adore his daughter, Sarah," Jillian said. "And she seems to like me." She laughed. "Though after his last wife, it's probably because she knows I have no need for her father's estate."

"I'm sure it's you Sarah likes. I can see you two getting along well."

"It's nice to have a pseudo daughter figure around." Then the look in Jillian's eyes turned calculated. "Though I had much preferred you."

Margot swallowed. "How is Clint?"

"Still waiting. I'm very proud of him for it. He doesn't do patience very well, nor is he good at relinquishing control of his relationships."

Though Margot was encouraged by the news, she didn't miss the insinuation in Jillian's words. The woman was telling her he wouldn't wait forever, and it brought back the paralyzing indecision Margot had been dealing with for weeks.

She so wanted to rush to him and beg herself back into his life, forgetting about her career and all her doubts and just acting on the ache in her heart. It would be so easy to live in the moment and do what felt right for today, worrying about tomorrow when tomorrow came. Thanks to Clint, she now understood why people made the mistakes they did, how easy it was to get caught up in their emotions.

But she'd seen from countless clients how disastrous it could be to ignore the deeper issues that always surfaced once the newness and excitement wore down. That was the place Margot was trying to avoid, but with every day that passed, it got harder and harder.

Jillian casually glanced around Margot's office. "And how are *you* doing?"

Margot opened her mouth to spill out the canned response that she was fine, but something in Jillian's expression wouldn't let her. Maybe it was the longing to have both of them back in her life. Maybe it was the knowing look in Jillian's eyes that said she already knew the answer without asking. But when Margot spoke, she couldn't stop from telling her the truth.

"I'm miserable."

Jillian didn't look surprised. "Of course, you are. You're in love with my son, but stubbornly staying away from him. What I don't understand is why."

She stared at Jillian, seeing so much of Clint in her eyes that Margot couldn't deny that those words were true. She was in love with Clint. She loved him with every last ounce of her heart. And trying to deny it was all but futile.

"I'm afraid of making a mistake," she admitted, boiling all the complications in her head down to that one simple truth.

"Why on earth would you think loving Clint is a mistake?"

It was the same question Margot continued to grapple with, and she kept going back to her four principles, the ones Rob had fit into far better than Clint. If one man was so right yet still wrong, how could the other even hope to last?

"We come from such different places," Margot tried to explain. "We aren't cut from the same cloth. If we'd filled out my surveys, I would have never put the two of us together. Too many things don't fit."

"Like what kinds of things? Income? Family background? Political beliefs?"

"Yes, all of those to start with."

"Goodness, I'm glad no one was around with surveys when Jerry and I met. He was a blue collar construction worker and I grew up in Beverly Hills. Jerry and the Colonel never even got along. In fact, I spent the bulk of my adult life working hard to keep them apart. Not to mention the fact that Jerry was a Baptist and I was Catholic, he was a liberal Democrat and my family was staunchly Republican. Yet through our thirty-five year marriage we were blissfully happy." She shook her head and sighed. "Who knew that during all those years we were supposed to have been all wrong for each other?"

Margot sat and stared, having nothing to say to that. Of course, she knew that people defied the odds every day. But most of them didn't. And those were the ones Margot saw on a daily basis. They were her constant reminder that without a fundamental common ground, most relationships failed.

"And come to think of it," Jillian added, "if that's the case, why did you put me together with Bo? He grew up a plumber's son in Detroit. You had to have known that."

Margot nodded.

"I mean, sure he's got money now. But our histories are entirely different, and as far as shared values, well, you don't even really know what my values are. It's not like I filled out one of your surveys."

"No, you didn't."

Margot bit her lip as the wheels began turning in her head. Tiny, rusty ones, revealing a small smidgen of awareness that rushed by too quickly to grasp. But she'd felt it. There was something here.

"So what made you think Bo and I would be so perfect for each other?" Jillian asked.

Margot shook her head. "I just had a hunch."

"A hunch? And is that the problem with Clint? You don't have a hunch about him?"

"I…" She struggled, not exactly certain. When it came to her and Clint all the connections between her head and her heart were so jumbled she didn't know what was up and what was down. Their relationship had been whirlwind. She'd never had the quiet she'd needed to really hear her instincts.

In fact, as she thought about it, she hadn't put much credence in her gut lately at all, that slump having put a dent in her faith that she'd never fully restored. Since then, she'd been relying on logic, experience and her years of schooling to get by.

All things tangible in a business that was anything but.

A sprout of awareness began to grow, still a whisper, but loud enough to tell Margot this was something she needed to pursue. Maybe it was the first piece to the puzzle she was trying to put back together. Or maybe it was a dead end. She didn't know. But for the first time in weeks, Jillian had given her something new to grasp, and she wasn't about to dismiss it.

"You might be on to something," she admitted.

"Margot, I've had a hunch about you since the first night we met. I think you and Clint belong together. I don't understand why you don't see it, too. This is your business, after all."

She stared at Jillian, the tiny wheels now gaining momentum. Could it be this easy? Was it that she'd stopped trusting her instincts? Jillian was right. When it came to pairing her up with Bo, Margot hadn't been able to rely on her surveys and questionnaires. She'd only had a few dinners to go by and was never able to ask too many pointed questions for fear of blowing her cover. Much like Margot had done before she'd started her business, she'd had to rely on her gut to tell her which man would be a good candidate.

And with Jillian and Bo she'd been spot-on, hadn't she?

This was it. This was the avenue she needed to go down. And she knew exactly what to do to prove her theory for sure.

"Oh, Jillian," she said, smiling with the first ray of hope she'd felt in a long time. "I think, thanks to you, I do see it."

17

"EDWARD, IT'S GOOD to see you." Clint held out a hand to his friend, Ed Mahoney, as he stepped into Ed's downtown Los Angeles office.

Clint had made the appointment to discuss a new project, a small four-home development north of Los Angeles, to seek Ed out as a possible partner. But before their time was up today, Clint intended to broach the subject of Ed's grandson, Brad, and Clint's need to get the kid off his shoulders. It would be tricky since every time Ed had inquired about Brad, Clint had claimed the boy was doing fine. In Clint's opinion, that had been diplomacy with a little wishful thinking tossed in. Margot had called it lying. And now that he found himself having to level with Ed face-to-face, he agreed Margot had been right.

This would be awkward, to say the least. But the Proctor mess had been the final straw after eight weeks of Brad-induced disasters. Clint had officially run out of things he could trust the kid to handle, and with the young man continually looking for excuses to cut out early every day, Clint would like to do them both the favor by not having him show up in the first place.

"How's your mother doing?" Ed asked as the two took seats at his conference table.

"Good. She's got a new man in her life, so I haven't seen as much of her lately. But when I do, she's happy."

Though quite a bit older than Clint's parents, Ed had been a longtime friend of the family, an early investor in H & H Associates who had put money into a number of their projects. And when Clint's father died, Ed had steadfastly stood behind Clint when others had shied away, fearing he didn't have the experience to keep the company profitable on his own.

Clint had done well, quickly regaining the confidence of most of his father's associates, but he would never forget the loyalty Ed had paid him during his roughest time. Which made this particular conversation even more difficult.

"I'd heard Jillian had started dating someone," Ed said. "The man's a stockbroker, is that right?"

"Yes."

Ed grinned. "Well, if he's making any money, I'd love to meet him."

Clint laughed. "I'm sure I can arrange that."

They made small talk while Ed's assistant brought in coffee, and as Clint expected, it didn't take long for the topic of Brad to come up.

"So is my grandson still working out for you?"

"Ed, that's one of the things I wanted to talk to you about." Clint tapped his fingers on the table and braced for the worst. "I've been trying my damnedest to give the boy a chance, but…" He stalled while he searched for a kind way to express his opinion of Brad. Nothing came to mind, and he found himself darting his gaze from Ed's expectant eyes as he fumbled to finish the sentence. "Brad's not exactly…he's…"

"I think the words you're searching for are unmotivated and inept," Ed offered.

Clint met Ed's knowing glance.

"Clint, I've been dealing with Brad since he was a baby. I know how he is."

"I am finding him a little devoid of ambition."

Ed threw his head back and laughed. "Son, if you ever get tired of contracting, there's a career for you in politics."

Clint couldn't keep the half smile from forming on his lips.

"It's true," Ed added. "Brad doesn't want to do anything that involves work. That's my daughter's fault. Brad's father was never in the picture, and I'm afraid Tammy overcompensated by spoiling the kid. Heck, we all did, now that I look back on it. He was the first grandson in the family. You know how it goes."

"I didn't know that about his father."

Ed sipped his coffee. "I would have said more about Brad when I asked you to take him on, but I didn't want to influence your opinion of him. You're the youngest executive I know, and I'd hoped maybe someone closer to his age could connect with him on a level the rest of us can't."

Clint shook his head. "I'm sorry—"

Ed held up a hand. "Don't be. You've done me a great favor giving him a chance and I owe you one. Besides, I confess that I was feeling inadequate when I'd thought Brad was working out well with you. God knows, I've tried more than a dozen times to find him a place in my organization." Ed chuckled lightheartedly. "My selfish side is glad to confirm it's not just me."

"No, it's not. And believe me, I gave Brad a shot at every job I could come up with. I really don't think he's cut out for the construction business."

"Nor any other occupation that I've found."

"Has he tried sales?" Clint remarked halfheartedly.

"Sales?"

Clint shrugged and considered his experience with Brad, telling Ed about the Proctor house and how convincing Brad had been in selling Proctor on that resort property.

"I think if you can find something he's passionate about, people would have a hard time saying no to him," Clint suggested, with honesty. "Real estate, cars—heck, set him up with a surf shop down in Malibu and he'd make you millions."

"You really think so?"

Clint hadn't exactly considered it before. He'd been too busy being angry with the kid and dodging Ed's inquiries. But looking at the situation objectively, Brad had pulled quite a feat in getting Proctor to do such an about-face.

"Yeah," Clint said, nodding. "I do." Then he joked, "Have someone do the books for him, for sure. I can't envision him remembering to lock up the cash register at night. But yes, if I were to steer him in a given direction, it would be sales of some sort. Preferably a field where he could make his own hours."

Ed looked genuinely intrigued and impressed, and the conversation had Clint wondering why he hadn't come here weeks ago. This discussion was a huge weight off his shoulders, and it appeared to be helping Ed, too. Clint should have known to come here sooner. It's what Margot had suggested and surely what his father would have advised if he'd still been alive. Clint hadn't done anyone any favors by beating around the bush and pretending things were fine when they weren't, and as he spent the next hour talking business with Ed, he became more convinced that it was time to start making some changes in his life.

Clint hadn't realized it before, but ever since his father died, he'd been on a wayward path, moving farther and farther from the man he was raised to be. Being left with the weight of his mother and the business to deal with on his own had put him in survival mode. Once he'd calmed everyone down and regained some normalcy in life, he'd been afraid to rock the boat for fear of losing it all. He'd started treading lightly, trying to keep his mother happy and his investors pleased and eager to do business with him to the point that he'd been afraid of making any move that might stir up conflict.

And in the end, all he'd done was make a mess of his life.

An hour after walking into Ed's office, he walked out deciding it was time to make some changes. He was through going passively through life catering to other people's timetables. It was already agreed with Ed that Brad's internship was over. As soon as Clint could arrange a final paycheck, he'd have a talk with the kid and send him on his way.

That would be one problem down. How many more to go?

As Clint got in his car and began the half-hour drive back to his office, he started chalking up a mental list. He was through with his mother as a permanent houseguest. Tears or no tears, it was time to set her up in a place of her own. He had no more doubts that she was ready to take on her new life, and he needed his privacy back so he could find a new life of his own.

Which brought him to his last issue. Margot.

As much as he'd like to play the patron saint, he couldn't go on putting his life on hold. If she hadn't figured out by now that they were meant for each other, more weeks of waiting wouldn't change that. So by the time he'd reached his office and made his way up the elevator, he'd come up with a new plan of action, one that didn't involve sitting around waiting for a woman to decide that she loved him. It was time to take charge again and deal with the consequences when they came.

Pushing through the glass doors with a new goal on his mind, he was met with Carmen's hesitant smile.

"So? How'd it go?" she asked.

He grabbed a bottle of water and then told her about his

meeting with Edward, giving her instructions to write up a final paycheck for Brad so he could talk to him before the day was out. Clint figured the sooner he got on board with his new plan, the better.

"I'd like to say I'm going to miss him," Carmen said. "But as interesting as he was to have around, I'd kind of like to get back to the quiet I'm accustomed to."

"It'll be even quieter after today. I'll be taking a few days off."

"That's sudden. Has something come up?"

"In a way. Do me a favor and cancel any appointments I've got through the end of the week." He started toward his office, then stopped. "And what was the name of that bed-and-breakfast you'd raved about last summer?"

"You mean the Bainbridge House up the coast?"

"That's it. Do you have their number? I'm curious to see if they've got a room through Sunday."

She looked at him quizzically as she brought up the number on her computer and jotted it on a pad. "Sure, but it's…kind of a place for couples."

He smiled and picked up the note. "Perfect."

Carmen regarded him with confusion until a wide grin formed on her face. "You heard from Margot!"

"No, I haven't," he said, draining the excitement in her eyes. "I'm done waiting on Margot."

"But—"

He held up the paper. "Thank you, Carmen." Then he tucked it in his pocket and headed for his office.

"Wow, you've had more clients than I remembered."

Margot looked up from her stacks of files as Alan stepped into her office and glanced around at all the folders. She'd spent the morning at their storage unit, pulling all her client files back to the day she'd started her business. Since then, she'd been poring through them, categorizing them into piles that were now spread all over her office.

"So are you finding what you hoped?" he asked.

"This is exactly it, Alan. Everything we discussed last night, it's all right here just like we suspected."

After her meeting with Jillian had got her thinking, she'd run her thoughts by Alan over drinks. He'd concurred with her feeling that she'd gotten too wrapped up in her surveys lately, dismissing her instinct over what she could calculate on a black-and-white page. It seemed so obvious now, so blatantly clear that she didn't know how she'd missed it all this time. And when she started running through her older files, she was left with no doubts.

"Look at this," she said, getting up from her desk and holding up two folders for Alan. "Remember Connie and Steve?"

Alan glanced at the files. "Yeah, the brunette who always dressed in black, right?"

"Yep. Look at their surveys. They're in roughly the same place when it comes to the four principles, but nowhere near a solid match. If I'd looked at these two a week ago, I would have never considered them for each other."

"So why did you then?"

She shrugged. "I just had a feeling. Talking to her, talking to him, I could see them together. They *felt* like they fit. And you know what? I called Connie this morning to check up on them and they're still doing great. They recently celebrated their second wedding anniversary and are happy as clams."

Snapping the folders closed, she stepped to her credenza and placed them on a stack. "All of these," she said, waving a hand over the piles. "These are the clients I would have never matched if I'd relied on their surveys alone. And of the ones I've been able to get in touch with, almost all are still together and going strong."

Margot looked over her towers of success, as she'd coined them, feeling as though the weight of the world had risen off her chest leaving her giddy and excited. Over the last few months, her friends and family had told her to keep the faith, but up until now, the idea hadn't really locked in her mind. But in the end, that's what all her problems had boiled down to. She'd lost faith. And to get her business back on track, all she needed to do was trust her instincts.

"That's pretty compelling," Alan said. "Is it giving you ideas about changing direction with some of your current clients?"

"A few. And I'm not expecting a smooth road back. I need to rethink every one of them and prepare myself for some bumps. But I have the answer I've been looking for and a solid idea for a new direction."

He smiled. "It's nice to see you happy again. The cloud of gloom over this place had gotten so dark, I was about to dig out my umbrella."

Margot laughed. She *was* happy, and not only because of her business. Once she'd sat and reflected on where she'd gone wrong, everything fell into place, including her love life. Though she didn't agree with Rob's method of handling things, when it came to their relationship, Margot had to admit he'd been right. They'd gotten along wonderfully, like comfy old friends, but there wasn't a solitary spark between them.

Margot had known that, or rather her subconscious had known it from the start. And now that she saw it clearly, she knew the unease she'd felt about them had been the source of her anxiousness when it came to their relationship. She'd felt the need to rush with Rob, at the time believing it was because she'd found Mr. Right. But now, standing back, she saw that it was because her heart was trying to tell her they were wrong, and her head didn't want to listen.

But she was listening now. And with her mind freed and her trust gradually reforming, she knew exactly what had been wrong with Rob, and more importantly, what was so right about Clint.

She reflected back on her conversation with Jillian the day before, what Jillian had said about her thirty-five-year marriage to Jerry. They'd so obviously complemented each other, not because they matched, but because they balanced. They weren't two of the same, but instead, two halves of one whole.

Exactly the way Margot felt about Clint.

Her heart had been telling her since the moment he stepped into her office that he was the man for her. The spark had been there, the respect, the friendship. So the four principles hadn't aligned tightly, but as Margot reflected back on her original thesis, they were never supposed to. They were only a guideline, the more important aspects of a relationship being the spiritual chemistry between two people that couldn't be measured on paper.

It was the talent for seeing that in others that had made Margot good at her job. And as she allowed herself to look at it for her own life, she could see how perfectly that chemistry balanced between her and Clint.

It was the basis for love. And right now, her heart brimmed with it.

"So what are you going to do to celebrate?" Alan asked.

"I'm thinking a surprise." And an apology. And a lifetime of thanks to Clint for having enough faith to carry them both while she figured this out for herself.

"A surprise?"

She grinned and checked her watch. "Yep. Right now, I need to see a man about my future."

She figured Clint would still be at work for at least another hour. Typically, even if he had a meeting or went to one of the job sites, he stopped back in the office at the end of the day to sign papers or lock up. And if things worked in her favor, she'd catch him before he left.

So asking Alan to wish her luck, she shut down her laptop and headed straight to Clint's office. She considered doing something special, maybe stopping for a gift, quickly running home and changing into something a little racier, but realized she didn't have the patience to wait a minute longer. She wanted Clint in her arms and back in her life, beginning the first day of what she hoped would be a lifetime with the man she loved.

And she wanted it now.

Her heart sped as she hit Wilshire Boulevard and found a place to park. What should she say? What would be her first words? Or should she simply let her body do the talking with a long, sensual and totally overdue kiss?

That might not be appropriate if she were to walk in and find him occupied in a meeting or maybe standing in Carmen's front office. But maybe she wouldn't care. Maybe an audience would enhance the emotion, providing a witness to her profession of love and urging him to accept her apology for making him wait as long as he did.

She couldn't decide, so she figured she'd go with the moment and hope she didn't freeze when she looked into those stunning blue eyes and caught her first glimpse of the man who represented her future happiness.

It was that thought that put a wide grin on her face as she stepped through the doors and found Carmen sitting at her desk.

"Margot," Carmen said, apparently surprised to see her

show up unannounced. Margot admitted that spontaneity wasn't a trait she was famous for—something she intended to change going forward.

She gripped her purse, only now acknowledging how nervous she was about facing Clint after all these weeks. Or were her fingers trembling with excitement? She wasn't sure.

"Tell me Clint's here," she begged.

The stunned looked remained on Carmen's face. "No, he's not. What are you doing here?"

A thrill zipped up her spine as she blurted her news. "I figured it out, Carmen. I know what went wrong with my business. I figured out where I went wrong with Rob, and now I need to fix what I messed up with Clint. Where is he? Will he be back?"

Carmen's jaw bobbed before she said, "No. He's gone for the day. In fact, he won't be back until Monday."

Margot shrugged. "Okay. I'll go track him down at home."

Then she noted the look on Carmen's face.

"You don't seem too thrilled," she said, watching as the deer-in-the-headlights expression Carmen had been holding darkened to something grim. "What's wrong? Tell me."

"Oh, Margot," Carmen said, shaking her head. "Why couldn't you have figured this out yesterday?"

Margot's giddy excitement slipped a notch. "Yesterday? Why? Where's Clint?" Though as the look on Carmen's face began to sink in, she wasn't sure she wanted to know.

"He left before lunch. He's…" She ran a hand through her hair. "Why couldn't you have figured this out yesterday?"

"Left for where?"

Carmen opened her mouth but didn't speak, and Margot's gaze froze on her friend as everything right about her life just slipped out from under her.

She didn't have to ask any more questions. She knew what

Carmen was saying. Clint had moved on. Exactly as she'd feared. And for the second time in as many months, she found herself on the wrong end of yet another failure.

Except losing Clint wasn't simply another failure. It was devastating on a scale that made her experience with Rob seem like a minor inconvenience.

"He's gone?"

Carmen glanced at the clock. "I'm sure he's on his way out of town by now. Hon, he wasn't going alone."

Margot's throat closed up and she fought for air as Carmen quickly rushed from her desk to Margot's side. "Honey, I'm so sorry."

"Who? Where?" was all Margot could choke out.

Carmen placed an arm on Margot's shoulder. "Up the coast. He took the rest of the week off and wasn't coming back." She looked as though she were about to cry herself, and it was the last thing Margot needed to see.

Tears rushed to Margot's eyes and she stepped out of Carmen's grasp and headed toward the door. "I need to go."

"Margot, don't leave like this. Let me get my purse and I'll go with you."

Unable to face her friend, Margot shook her head and kept walking. "I'll be fine. I need to be alone."

"Margot, please."

"No. I'll call you later." Then she threw together the most strength she could muster and put on a good face. "I'll be fine, Carmen. Really. I just need to be alone."

Then without waiting for an answer, she rushed out the door and out of the building, a day late and one broken heart too many. She jabbed the button for the elevator and fought for breath, the crushing blow pressing against her chest and stealing the strength from her legs.

She'd lost Clint. She'd waited too long, stretched his

patience too far and passed the limits of what he was capable of giving her. The weight of it was only beginning to set in. And when she stepped out of the building into the warmth of the afternoon heat, she fell apart in a routine that had become all too familiar lately. Except this time, she hadn't simply made a stupid mistake with her heart.

This time, she'd lost the love of her life.

18

MARGOT PULLED UP to her condo and killed the engine, realizing only after the fact that she probably shouldn't have been driving. She supposed she should have taken Carmen up on her offer to drive her home, but she couldn't bear to hear any words of support. She knew what Carmen would say, how Margot was too good for Clint if he couldn't have waited for her to straighten out her problems. How he'd made a promise he didn't stand by. How all men are rats and pigs and she was better off without him.

It was Carmen's style, and right now, Margot didn't want to hear it. Because she knew without a doubt she had no one to blame but herself.

Clint had expressed his love for her and she'd thrown it back in his face, and, no matter what anyone said, she deserved what she got. Clint wasn't a rat or a pig. He was the best thing that had ever happened to her and she'd tossed him off as if his love were a burden instead of a gift. And for that, she'd never forgive herself.

Resting her arms on the steering wheel, she buried her face in her hands, wondering how she would ever get over what she'd done. On her way home, she'd almost turned the car around and gone to track him down, ready to burst in on him and whomever he was with and beg him to give her one more chance.

But she'd chickened out and decided that she'd humiliated herself often enough lately. Besides, she'd really, truly created this situation. Now it was hers to live with.

Pulling her keys from the ignition, she clutched them in her hand, grabbed her purse and stepped out of the car. Her legs felt heavy, her body ached, and all she wanted to do now was get to her couch where she'd spend the rest of the evening wishing she could turn back the clock. Grief consumed her, the sorrow, anger and self-loathing sinking her to such a depth that she didn't even see the figure standing in her path until she bumped straight into him.

"Whoa," he said grasping her arms, and when she looked up her heart nearly stopped.

Clint!

His surprise immediately turned to concern. "Margot, what's wrong?"

"You're—" She couldn't speak, the breath sucked from her lungs at the sight of him.

He brushed the hair from her face. "Baby, what happened?"

She shook her head, too confused and surprised to form words. What was he doing here? Carmen said he'd taken off, that he'd moved on. The look on her face had been unmistakable. She'd said—Margot searched her brain—what exactly had Carmen said?

"Why are you crying like this?" he asked.

"I stopped by your office," she blubbered. "Carmen—"

Understanding dawned and relaxed the worry in his eyes. He cupped her face in his hands. "Babe, there's never going to be another woman for me. That's what I came here to tell you."

"You what?"

Pulling her into an embrace, he held her close and brushed

his fingers through her hair. "You're mine, Margot. There's no other woman for me and there never will be."

New tears filled her eyes, but these were good ones. "I showed up to tell you I love you," she blurted, sliding her hands up his back and burying her face in the warmth of his chest. "I thought that you were taking off with someone."

He kissed her head. "You were the one I was leaving with."

"Me?"

"Yes." He clasped her shoulders and nudged her back to look her in the eye. "I came to tell you I'm done waiting on you. That you owe me that weekend you promised me, and by the end of it you're going to be mine, like it or not." He pressed his lips to hers, the simple touch spilling sensation through her veins that, just a moment ago, she hadn't expected to ever feel again.

"But I've made a compromise," he said, smiling. "Instead of the high-class resorts and expensive yachts, I booked four nights at a cozy B&B up the coast."

"To make me yours," she repeated, sniffing away her sorrow to make room for pure joy.

"To make you mine."

She tightened her arms around him and pulled him close. "I already am yours." She kissed his lips. "I have been since the day we met." She kissed him again, then whispered, "And I'd come to tell you I love you." Then she choked back a giggle, still dizzy over the fact that he was here, and he loved her, and she hadn't blown the best thing that had ever happened to her.

He responded with a long slow smile as he embraced her, his body spreading delight everywhere it snuggled against hers. "I love you, too, babe. I always will."

And with those simple words, every aspect of her life righted itself and aligned in perfect unison. Her career, her love life, both so intertwined by the nature of what she did that she hadn't been able to work out one without the other. But now they'd come together as a whole, restoring her faith in love and her trust in herself.

She'd had a hunch about Clint Hilton, and as he held her face in his hands and consumed her with a sweet, tender kiss, she knew that the most important principle was the one she felt in her heart.

Epilogue

One Year Later

CLINT STOOD at the chapel and watched as the bride approached the aisle. She was beautiful. More stunning than he'd ever seen her before, dressed in a simple ivory gown adorned with small pearl beads that matched her jewelry.

With every step she took, his heart filled, happy that he and his family had come this far after the loss of his father just a few years ago. It had been a hard and bumpy ride for everyone, and this wedding marked the first of many new beginnings. Within a year or two, the Hiltons would no doubt be welcoming a new generation as families joined and children were born.

Nate had surprised them all by coming home for the wedding, a new woman on his arm and plans to come back to the States for good. His foreign travels had been an experience of a lifetime, but love with a journalist who had taken a job in New York had brought him back to the U.S. with the intent to stay.

Funny how love had a way of bringing everything full circle.

Clint took the bride's hand as she stepped to his side. He pressed a kiss to her cheek and asked, "You ready?"

"I think so," his mother said.

"We can turn and run," he joked. "Margot and I came in the Porsche. Zero to sixty in four-point-seven seconds."

She squeezed his hand. "You'd never let me. Bo's the best thing that's happened to you, admit it."

"No. Margot's the best thing that's happened to me. Nate coming home is second. Bo, I'm afraid, brings up the rear in third." Clint winked. "I am thankful for him, though. He'll make you happy."

She took a nervous breath as the music began playing, signaling it was time to walk down the aisle. "You sure about that?"

"Of course. Margot said so."

The procession began and the ceremony went off without a hitch, transforming Jillian Hilton into Mrs. Jillian Granger, though Clint knew a part of her would always be a Hilton, just like a part of her had never stopped being Jillian Chamberlain.

Afterward, they all traveled to Bo's country club for the reception, and as Clint rested by the bar, he watched as Margot and Bo's daughter, Sarah, busied themselves, making sure everything happened smoothly. It was almost an hour into the festivities before he could catch her alone on the dance floor and steal some time for themselves.

"So when are we going to have one of these?" he asked, holding her in his arms while the band played the old 1950s song "You Send Me."

She looked stunning in a grape-colored taffeta dress that crisscrossed her chest, slipped snugly around her waist and curved around her hips where it stopped just above the knee. Studying the construction, he decided the best thing about it was how easily it would come off. Now that she'd moved in with him, he was haunted with the knowledge of what she was wearing underneath—a new hazard of living under the same roof.

"Are you asking me to marry you?" she said.

He moved lazily to the music, enjoying the feel of her body pressed against his.

"Nope. When I do that, it will be in a very private and romantic setting. I'll have a nice speech planned out and a big gaudy ring in my pocket. Right now, I'm just feeling you out."

She raised a brow. "A big gaudy ring, huh?"

"You'll be too embarrassed to wear it."

She smiled, and it did funny things to his stomach. He wondered if he'd ever get over the flutters he always got any time she was near.

"Don't sell me short. I'm getting good at gaudy."

He laughed, knowing it was true. One thing Margot was only now learning about his mother was that the woman had some fairly outrageous decorating tastes. If it was gilded or French—preferably both—his mother loved it, and Margot was getting her fill of the style helping Jillian decorate the new house she and Bo had bought. They'd found the home through Brad Mahoney, of all people, acting out of friendship for Ed as one of Brad's first clients in the real estate business.

Apparently, the kid had taken Clint's advice and had actually obtained his Realtor's license, signing on with a small but respectable brokerage firm. And to everyone's surprise, he was doing well.

It amazed Clint how far every aspect of his life had come in such a short time. His mother was now remarried, starting the first few pages of the next chapter of her life. Nate had come home, and though he planned to settle in New York, it was much closer than Afghanistan and eased everyone's worries. Margot had become a permanent fixture in Clint's life. And even though they'd yet to make it official, he knew that was only a matter of time. She'd sold her condo and made her home with him, and he knew once this wedding was over, they'd be busy planning one of their own.

Funny how only a year ago he'd been struggling alone, working hard to keep things together. And now he was surrounded by love and family, the best of it all right here in his arms.

"I love you more than anything," he said. And when she looked up and met his gaze, the words meant a little more than the daily reminders he tossed out. This time, they sunk in just that bit further.

Some would tell him it was the romance of the setting, or the joyous celebration, or being surrounded by friends and family. But Clint knew it wasn't the champagne bringing him that warm feeling inside. It was Margot. The one woman who came in and filled all the gaps in his life and in his spirit. It felt good and whole, bringing him a level of happiness he never dreamed was possible.

And as they moved along the dance floor to the slow, sexy beat of the song, he knew this was something he would hold on to forever.

* * * * *

RICK'S APPOINTMENT with his attorney early Wednesday morning went only moderately better than his meeting with social services the day before. The prognosis wasn't great—but at least his attorney was going to file a motion for DNA testing. Just so Rick could petition to see the child…his sister's baby. The sister he didn't know he had until it was too late.

The rest of what his attorney said had been downhill from there.

Cell phone in hand before he'd even reached his Nitro, Rick punched in the speed dial number he'd programmed the day before.

Maybe foster parent Sue Bookman hadn't received his message. Or had lost his number. Maybe she didn't want to talk to him. At this point he didn't much care what she wanted.

"Hello?" She answered before the first ring was complete. And sounded breathless.

Young and breathless.

"Ms. Bookman?"

"Yes. This is Rick Kraynick, right?"

"Yes, ma'am."

"I recognized your number on caller ID," she said, her voice uneven, as though she was still engaged in whatever physical activity had her so breathless to begin with. "I'm sorry I didn't get back to you. I've been a little…distracted."

The words came in more disjointed spurts. Was she jogging?

"No problem," he said, when, in fact, he'd spent the better part of the night before watching his phone. And fretting. "Did I get you at a bad time?"

"No worse than usual," she said, adding, "Better than some. So, how can I help?"

God, if only this could be so easy. He'd ask. She'd help. And life could go well. At least for one little person in his family.

It would be a first.

"Mr. Kraynick?"

"Yes. Sorry. I was…are you sure there isn't a better time to call?"

"I'm bouncing a baby, Mr. Kraynick. It's what I do."

"Is it Carrie?" he asked quickly, his pulse racing.

"How do you know Carrie?" She sounded defensive, which wouldn't do him any good.

"I'm her uncle," he explained, "her mother's—Christy's— older brother, and I know you have her."

"I can neither confirm nor deny your allegations, Mr. Kraynick. Please call social services." She rattled off the number.

"Wait!" he said, unable to hide his urgency. "Please," he said more calmly. "Just hear me out."

"How did you find me?"

"A friend of Christy's."

"I'm sorry I can't help you, Mr. Kraynick," she said softly. "This conversation is over."

"I grew up in foster care," he said, as though that gave him some special privilege. Some insider's edge.

"Then you know you shouldn't be calling me at all."

"Yes… But Carrie is my niece," he said. "I need to see her. To know that she's okay."

"You'll have to go through social services to arrange that."

"I'm sure you know it's not as easy as it sounds. I'm a single man with no real ties and I've no intention of petitioning for custody. They aren't real eager to give me the time of day. I never even knew Carrie's mother. For all intents and purposes, our mother didn't raise either one of us. All I have going for me is half a set of genes. My lawyer's on it, but it could be weeks—months—before this is sorted out. Carrie could be adopted by then. Which would be fine, great for her, but then I'd have lost my chance. I don't want to take her. I won't hurt her. I just have to see her."

"I'm sorry, Mr. Kraynick, but…"

* * * * *

Find out if Rick Kraynick will ever have a
chance to meet his niece.
Look for A DAUGHTER'S TRUST
by Tara Taylor Quinn,
available in September 2009.

**We'll be spotlighting a different series
every month throughout 2009
to celebrate our 60th anniversary.**

**Look for Harlequin® Superromance®
in September!**

*Celebrate with
The Diamond Legacy
miniseries!*

Follow the stories of four cousins as they come to terms
with the complications of love and what it means to
be a family. Discover with them the sixty-year-old secret
that rocks not one but two families.

A DAUGHTER'S TRUST by *Tara Taylor Quinn*
September

FOR THE LOVE OF FAMILY by *Kathleen O'Brien*
October

LIKE FATHER, LIKE SON by *Karina Bliss*
November

A MOTHER'S SECRET by *Janice Kay Johnson*
December

Available wherever books are sold.

www.eHarlequin.com

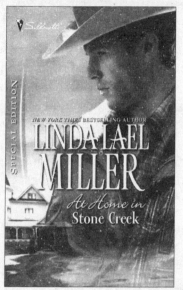

SILHOUETTE SPECIAL EDITION

FROM *NEW YORK TIMES* BESTSELLING AUTHOR

Ashley O'Ballivan had her heart broken by a man years ago—and now he's mysteriously back. Jack McCall *isn't* the person she thinks he is. For her sake, he must keep his distance, but his feelings for her are powerful. To protect her—from his enemies and himself—he has to leave...vowing to fight his way home to her and Stone Creek forever.

Available in November wherever books are sold.

SSE65487

You're invited to join our Tell Harlequin Reader Panel!

By joining our new reader panel you will:

- Receive Harlequin® books—they are FREE and yours to keep with no obligation to purchase anything!
- Participate in fun online surveys
- Exchange opinions and ideas with women just like you
- Have a say in our new book ideas and help us publish the best in women's fiction

In addition, you will have a chance to win great prizes and receive special gifts!
See Web site for details. Some conditions apply.
Space is limited.

To join, visit us at

www.TellHarlequin.com.

Tell HARLEQUIN

REQUEST YOUR FREE BOOKS!

2 FREE NOVELS
PLUS 2
FREE GIFTS!

HARLEQUIN®

Blaze™

Red-hot reads!

YES! Please send me 2 FREE Harlequin® Blaze™ novels and my 2 FREE gifts (gifts are worth about $10). After receiving them, if I don't wish to receive any more books, I can return the shipping statement marked "cancel." If I don't cancel, I will receive 6 brand-new novels every month and be billed just $4.24 per book in the U.S. or $4.71 per book in Canada. That's a savings of 15% off the cover price. It's quite a bargain. Shipping and handling is just 50¢ per book.* I understand that accepting the 2 free books and gifts places me under no obligation to buy anything. I can always return a shipment and cancel at any time. Even if I never buy another book, the two free books and gifts are mine to keep forever.

151 HDN EYS2 351 HDN EYTE

Name	(PLEASE PRINT)	
Address		Apt. #
City	State/Prov.	Zip/Postal Code

Signature (if under 18, a parent or guardian must sign)

Mail to the **Harlequin Reader Service:**
IN U.S.A.: P.O. Box 1867, Buffalo, NY 14240-1867
IN CANADA: P.O. Box 609, Fort Erie, Ontario L2A 5X3

Not valid to current subscribers of Harlequin Blaze books.

Want to try two free books from another line?
Call 1-800-873-8635 or visit www.morefreebooks.com.

Terms and prices subject to change without notice. Prices do not include applicable taxes. N.Y. residents add applicable sales tax. Canadian residents will be charged applicable provincial taxes and GST. Offer not valid in Quebec. This offer is limited to one order per household. All orders subject to approval. Credit or debit balances in a customer's account(s) may be offset by any other outstanding balance owed by or to the customer. Please allow 4 to 6 weeks for delivery. Offer available while quantities last.

Your Privacy: Harlequin Books is committed to protecting your privacy. Our Privacy Policy is available online at www.eHarlequin.com or upon request from the Reader Service. From time to time we make our lists of customers available to reputable third parties who may have a product or service of interest to you. If you would prefer we not share your name and address, please check here. ☐

HB09R3

Stay up-to-date on all your romance reading news!

The Harlequin Inside Romance newsletter is a **FREE** quarterly newsletter highlighting our upcoming series releases and promotions!

Go to
eHarlequin.com/InsideRomance
or e-mail us at
InsideRomance@Harlequin.com
to sign up to receive
your **FREE** newsletter today!

HARLEQUIN *Blaze*™

COMING NEXT MONTH

Available August 25, 2009

#489 GETTING PHYSICAL Jade Lee

For American student/waitress Zoe Lewis, Tantric sex—sex as a spiritual experience—is a totally foreign concept. Strange, yet irresistible. Then she's partnered with Tantric master Stephen Chiu…and discovers just how far great sex can take a girl!

#490 MADE YOU LOOK Jamie Sobrato
Forbidden Fantasies

She spies with her little eye… From the privacy of her living room Arianna Day has a front-row seat for her neighbor Noah Quinn's sex forays. And she knows he's the perfect man to end her bout of celibacy. Now to come up with the right plan to make him look…

#491 TEXAS HEAT Debbi Rawlins
Encounters

Four college girlfriends arrive at the Sugarloaf ranch to celebrate an engagement announcement. With all the tasty cowboys around, each will have a reunion weekend she'll never forget!

#492 FEELS LIKE THE FIRST TIME Tawny Weber
Dressed to Thrill

Zoe Gaston hated high school. So the thought of going back for her reunion doesn't exactly thrill her. Little does she guess that there's a really hot guy who's been waiting ten long years to do just that!

#493 HER LAST LINE OF DEFENSE Marie Donovan
Uniformly Hot!

Instructing a debutante in survival training is not how Green Beret Luc Boudreau planned to spend his temporary leave. Problem is, he kind of likes this feisty fish out of water and it turns out the feeling's mutual. But will they find any common ground other than their shared bedroll…?

#494 ONE GOOD MAN Alison Kent
American Heroes: The Texas Rangers

Jamie Danby needs a hero—badly. As the only witness to a brutal shooting, she's been flying below the radar for years. Now her cover's blown and she needs a sexy Texas Ranger around 24/7 to make her feel safe. The best sex of her life is just a bonus!